GAME MISCONDUCT

UTAH FURY HOCKEY BOOK 13

BRITTNEY MULLINER

D1520734

Game
MISCONDUCT
UTAH FURY HOCKEY BOOK THIRTEEN

This is a work of fiction. Names, characters, organizations, places, events, and incidents are either products of the author's imagination or are used fictitiously.

Copyright © 2021 Brittney Mulliner

All rights reserved.

ISBN-13: 979-8503831733

No part of this book may be reproduced, or stored in a retrieval system, or transmitted in any form or by any means, electronic, mechanical, photocopying, recording, or otherwise, without express written permission of the author.

ALSO BY BRITTNEY MULLINER

ROMANCE

Utah Fury Hockey

Puck Drop (Reese and Chloe)

Match Penalty (Erik and Madeline)

Line Change (Noah and Colby)

Attaching Zone (Wyatt and Kendall)

Buzzer Beater (Colin and Lucy)

Open Net (Olli and Emma)

Full Strength (Grant and Addison)

Drop Pass (Nikolay and Elena)

Scoring Chance (Derrek and Amelia)

Penalty Kill (Brandon and Sydney)

Power Play (Jason and Taylor)

Center Ice (Jake and Dani)

Game Misconduct (Parker and Vivian)

Face Off (Mikey and Holly)

Snowflakes & Ice Skates (Lance and Jessica)

A Holiday Short Story to be read between Center Ice and Game
Misconduct

Royals of Lochland

His Royal Request

His Royal Regret

Her Royal Rebellion

Young Adult

Begin Again Series

Begin Again

Live Again

Love Again (Coming Soon)

Charmed Series

Finding My Charming

Finding My Truth (Coming Soon)

Standalones

The Invisibles

For exclusive content and the most up to date news, sign up for Brittney's Reader's club at www.brittneymulliner.com

To Whitney,
for always getting me through

GAME MISCONDUCT

Rule 404 (b)

A "GAME MISCONDUCT" penalty involves the suspension of a player or Team Official for the balance of the game with immediate substitution taking place on ice.

https://www.usahockeyrulebook.com/

1

VIVIAN

The moment I stepped into my apartment, I could sense something was off.

"Duck!"

Growing up with three brothers taught me to react quickly to that word. I bent my knees and covered my head with my free arm as a football soared mere inches above me before slamming into the wall.

"I told you to take the ball outside," Jessica, my roommate, chastised the guys from the kitchen.

"It's too cold," her boyfriend, Lance, whined from the opposite side of the room.

"Then improve your aim," I called to him with a half-hearted glare as I hung my purse on a hook and shed my jacket, scarf, beanie, and gloves. Walking to work was a luxury that helped me save money on a car payment, gas, and insurance, but days like this, when the temperature wouldn't break freezing, made me regret the decision I'd made last summer.

"Hear that, Kirkpatric? Even Viv knows you suck." Mikey

Dankowski grinned and winked at me as I passed through the danger zone to the kitchen.

Jessica offered an apologetic smile along with a teriyaki steak bowl. "They got you dinner in hopes of softening you up."

"For what?" I asked as I pulled off the lid. The sweet and savory scent hit my nose, instantly making my mouth water. Work had been too busy for me to take a break for lunch, so the bribe was timed perfectly.

"They want to host a little party here, and I told them they have to clear it with you too."

I eyed the guys while I chewed. They continued to clumsily toss the ball back and forth. It was a good thing it wasn't a reflection of their skills with sticks and pucks, otherwise the Fury would have a very bleak outlook for playoffs.

It was beyond strange to even be thinking about hockey, a world I paid very little attention to before about two months ago when Jessica moved in. I've never been much of a sports person in general, but I at least knew the basics of basketball and football. Jessica and her boss, Dani, gave me lessons when they watched the away games here, but the learning curve was dramatic. Every time I thought I understood, icing or off-sides was called and I would have no idea why.

"A little party?" That sounded suspicious. It wasn't that I necessarily cared if they had people over, but making the guys work for it held the opportunity for entertainment.

"I doubt the whole team will come. Most of them have families they'd rather spend their time with, so it would probably only be a handful." Jess would know. She was close friends with many of the wives and girlfriends of the players from her connection with both Chloe Murray and Dani Glisten. I almost wish I'd known about her friend group before agreeing to be roommates. Jess, on her own, was great. Her outgoing personality balanced out my more introverted tendencies. They spent time together, but not so much that it felt like she didn't have her own space or privacy.

It was the addition of the constant flow of professional athletes that made me uncomfortable.

"What usually happens at these parties?" I asked after I swallowed another bite.

"Dinner, talking, just hanging out." Jess waved a dismissive hand.

The thought of feeding and entertaining an undetermined amount of people––famous people––was daunting, but it wasn't really my responsibility. For Jess, it was just another night. She planned elaborate events far more imposing and impressive as a career.

Lance and Mikey set the football on the couch and positioned themselves across from me with the most serious expressions I'd seen on either of them.

"Vivian," Lance started.

"Ms. Ashwood," Mikey corrected.

"*Lady* Ashwood." Lance shot his friend a victorious look while I waited for them to get to their question. "We bequeath you a favor."

"You're giving me a favor?" I asked with raised brows. "Wow, I can think of so many things I want."

Lance's eyes widened and he turned to Mikey, who shrugged. "It sounded fancy."

"I think you were thinking of beseech," Jess said with a giggle.

The guys slapped each other's arms while whispering blames at one another. When they refocused, Mikey spoke. "We would like to beseech a favor. The fellow men on the team invite everyone over for dinners every week or so, depending on our travel schedule, and neither of us has ever hosted. We desire to, but behold it saddens us to admit neither of us has the space to accommodate more than four or five people."

I'd never been to either of their homes, but it was hard to believe ours was significantly bigger. The living room and kitchen area were open-concept, and we had a larger than average balcony with a grill, but it was too cold to use the outside for a party.

"What will be required of me?" I continued in their attempt at formal language.

"Nothing." Lance straightened. "We will take care of set up, food, and clean up."

"All you have to do is sit back and enjoy," Mikey agreed with a vigorous nod.

I was invited? It hadn't been implied, and I didn't want to assume I'd be included in a team event, but I shouldn't have been surprised. They were great about making sure I felt welcome to join their plans. Jess even invited me along on dates, not that I ever accepted. It was nice that they offered though.

Just because I hang out with all the guys from one of the city's professional sports teams didn't mean I was lonely and bored all the time. My best friend, Kerry, was also my coworker. We applied for positions at the same time and were both hired as assistants to the two owners of a technology company. Neither of us grew up dreaming of these jobs, but they were great stepping stones while we figured out our real passions.

My parents weren't exactly thrilled that their only daughter went to school to become an assistant, but they said as long as I was happy, then they would be too. I did have a feeling my dad would show up in a year or two to remind me of my degree in computer science and how I could be making so much more if I worked as a developer. The problem was that I worked at a tech company that I could easily slide into a position that used by degree, but I didn't love coding or programming. I liked interacting with people too much to stare at a screen for eight solid hours each day.

"What say ye?" Lance asked with pleading eyes.

"What night are you thinking?" I dropped the fancy act.

"Friday?" Lance asked cautiously, as if he expected me to say no.

"Sounds good." I picked up the bowl and finished eating while they high-fived and moved back to the living room to discuss plans.

"Thanks for that," Jess said. "This is really important to them, and Lance's apartment is truly tiny. I think Mikey might be embarrassed to invite people over to his place. He has one sofa, a TV, and a coffee table. There's no dining room table or anywhere to eat besides the couch."

I chuckled. "Sounds like the ideal bachelor pad."

She laughed with me. "It really is. Neither of them has bothered decorating. All Lance has is a few framed jerseys, but they've been leaning against the walls for as long as I've known him. He said once that he was going to hang them but he needs a hammer and nails, so I'm not holding my breath."

"I could understand that if he hadn't lived here for very long or thought he might get traded, but he's been here for a while, right?"

"A few years," she confirmed.

Living in a blank space with nothing personal or homey would be depressing for me. I loved coming home at the end of the day to a place that felt comfortable and familiar.

She rolled her shoulders before tilting her head from side to side with a cringe.

"Still sore?" I asked as I crossed the space to throw away the trash.

"Yeah, Dani said I might be for a day or so, but I didn't expect it to be this bad."

When I got home the night before Jess was sprawled on the couch after getting a massage from someone her boss recommended. She said it hurt to move and even needed my help getting up to go to bed.

"I've been tender where there was a knot or where they applied more pressure, but never like this." I eyed her. "I wonder if you should go back."

Her eyes widened. "Oh no. I'm never going back."

I hid my smile. I didn't want to laugh at her pain, but her newfound fear was a bit entertaining.

"Maybe try a new place next time, or ask for gentle pressure."

She nodded. "Lesson learned."

"I can help." Lance wagged his brows as he passed them to get to the fridge. He pulled out the water filter pitcher Jess insisted on and filled a glass.

"No, you should talk to Amelia or Madi. They probably know someone that can help," Mikey suggested.

I recognized the names as wives of their teammates, but I hadn't met either of them.

"That's a good idea," Jess agreed and pulled out her phone.

"We're thinking of inviting all the newer guys as well as any of the single ones," Lance said with a grin in my direction.

I narrowed my eyes. "Okay."

"Just thought you would like to know," he replied, trying and failing to sound casual.

Mikey couldn't meet my gaze. They were planning something. I could sense it. That was another talent I developed as a part of surviving my brothers. I didn't think it was malicious, as most of the plots of my childhood had been, but it still made me uncomfortable.

Maybe they were like Jess, thinking that since I was

single, I would want to meet some of the eligible men on the team. Mikey was one of them, and I liked him well enough but only as a friend.

"Yeah! We'll be sure to introduce you to them," Lance added.

Now would be the best time to invent an excuse and pretend like I was busy on Friday. It was only three days away, so the short notice would work in my favor, but from the past month or so I'd learned they were relentless. Ninety percent of the time they could be distracted by turning on the TV or the mention of a ball, but when they really set their mind to something, they didn't let anything stop them. Apparently, I was the next object of obsession.

"Can't wait." I gave them a hint of a smile to help sell my lie.

It was a waste of breath to try to talk them out of it. I'd go through the motions of greeting strangers who were in my home, making sure nothing was damaged or destroyed, all while playing the part of the fun roommate, but I wasn't sure what those two thought would happen. They could introduce me to all the single players in the league, and it wouldn't matter.

From what I'd gathered from meeting the hockey wives, there was one specific commonality. Each woman was gorgeous, thin, and stylish. Granted, there was some diversity in the woman as far as what they wore and how skinny they were—some did actually have some curves—but it wasn't hard to put together that there was a type of woman the players went for.

Through years of practicing self-love and differentiating between healthy and skinny, I was quite confident in who I was and how I looked, which was how I could accept that I was not the players' type without crying or hating my body.

I didn't let my dress size influence my happiness. I ate

well, although I did have a weakness for quality cake I didn't bother to hide, and I exercised a few times a week. What mattered was that my doctor agreed I was healthy and loved myself.

I didn't say anything aloud, but I was perfectly aware that their efforts were in vain. I accepted my role as *the friend* years ago. That's all I was to Mikey and Lance, and once they introduced me to their teammates, I'd become their *friend* too. At least Jess was already dating Lance. The worst was being used by a man in order to get with one of my friends. I went through that far too many times in high school and college until I realized I didn't have to keep letting it happen. Learning to stand up for myself and not letting myself get used had been a painful lesson to learn, and I was glad to be past that stage of life.

2

PARKER

There were worse situations. There had to be. In the grand scheme of things, this was one blip. A blink. I'd forget all about this in a few months or years. I jumped away from the rustling sound coming from the overflowing trash cans that stood on either side of the back entrance to my new apartment building. The slightly less offensive front entrance had a metal grate door with a lock I didn't own a key to.

This door was unlocked, presumably always, since it hung a bit crooked and the latch didn't match up to the hole. Was this really suitable for human residents? I glanced inside the dark corridor, but even with the sunlight filling in from behind me, I couldn't see much beyond the first ten feet. I stroked my beard, a habit I picked up since it grew longer over the past year, and considered alternatives. Sleeping in my car suddenly seemed like a good idea. The coupe didn't have a backseat, but I'd make it work, at least until I could figure out where I was really supposed to live.

Or a hotel. Yeah, that was what I was going to do. I should have looked for one the second I pulled up to this place.

As soon as I had a free hand, I was calling my manager and firing him.

"Need some help?" a voice said too closely.

I spun in the slushy snow, tightening my grip on my bags, to find a grungy man with a hood pulled low over his head and thin sweats with suspicious stains covering the front. I took a step back.

"No, thank you." I eased back into the building, and the man followed me. "I'm really fine."

"I insist." His hand reached out, and I caught a flash of silver and diamonds on his hand. It looked like a championship ring.

I studied him closer and realized the hoodie he was wearing had a discrete Fury logo on the left sleeve. My shoulders slumped. This was some sort of sick hazing ritual.

I muttered, *thanks* under my breath and handed him one of my bags. "I really appreciate your help, man."

He held my bag in midair and cocked his head. "You're really just going to hand over your stuff?"

I managed to hold back a laugh and let him think his ruse was still working. "Yeah, I'm exhausted, and I could use a free hand. I forgot what number I'm in."

I pulled out my phone and opened the most recent text from Omar, my manager. "Three-eleven." I looked around the hall for any sign of an elevator or staircase.

"You shouldn't trust strangers." He sounded confused.

"I don't, but I do trust my teammates," I said without looking at him.

He hmphed and pulled his hood back, revealing Mitch Doranon's famously ginger hair. "How'd you know?"

I chuckled. "I don't know many robbers that have Stanley Cup rings and team merch." I tilted my chin toward the logo on his upper arm.

He frowned. "Dang, Parker. I should have been more thorough."

"Why are you wearing your ring when you're ..." I looked over his clothing again. "Working on your car?"

Mitch laughed. "I was at the boxing gym. One of the guys asked to see the ring last week, and I remembered today."

I shook my head. I'd heard stranger stories, and it wasn't really my business. "Do you live here?"

His eyes widened. "No. No one does."

I glanced around the dilapidated hallway. "That's comforting." But this was the address Omar sent me, so something wasn't adding up.

"Come on. I'll show you to the right place." Mitch carried my bag and led the way down the alley half a block to a building that looked like it successfully passed its last inspection, to my relief.

"I don't understand. My manager sent me--"

"Happens all the time with those map apps. For some reason, our address goes there. Someone guessed that the street was renumbered or something. Chloe texted me and said you would be arriving around eleven, and I tried to get here before you, but this worked out." He laughed. "But I promise this is the right place."

Through all of that only one word stuck out to me. "Our?"

He smiled over his shoulder as he led me through a clean, bright hall to a shining silver elevator door. "Yeah, you're my new roommate."

I blinked. Roommate? I hadn't had a roommate since I was eighteen and playing in the major juniors, seven years ago. None of this was making sense. Was this still a part of the joke?

Mitch continued speaking as we took the elevator to the third floor. "Chloe called me and asked if I minded you moving into one of my spare rooms since it was all so last minute. Coach Romney and Rust thought you would like to live with one of us rather than staying in a hotel while you get settled. Things have been a little too quiet since Atkinson got traded, so I said yes."

Huh. Another detail my manager forgot to tell me. I needed to start asking more questions on our calls.

He stopped at the door marked three-eleven, unlocked it, and held it open for me to walk in first. "I would have wanted to have a roommate when I first moved here. Someone to show me around, not just with the team and the area, but the city. Salt Lake is great. There are a ton of restaurants and shopping, if you're into that."

He had a good point. While I didn't necessarily love the idea of living with a stranger, it would be nice to have someone close by for help. This was pretty common in the lower league, but not so much when you made it to the majors. Maybe our agents and managers were supposed to take over that role as guide, but since mine were located in Los Angeles, I wasn't sure they would be of much use.

"Make yourself at home. We have a few hours before practice, so you can unpack or rest. If you need anything, just holler." He stopped in front of the second door off the hall. "This one's yours."

I nodded, and he patted my shoulder as he walked back through the modern, clean living room where another door led to his bedroom. He kept the door open, and I stared for a second at the piles of clothes next to the unmade bed and stacks of jerseys and posters with his face in the back corner before turning back to my own. In the center of the room, a queen bed was covered with a dark red comforter with matching nightstands on either side, and a dresser stood against the wall. I pulled my bags over the gray hardwood and went to the sliding mirror doors to check out the closet.

It wasn't huge, but it was enough space for the few items that needed to be hung up. One of the perks of being a professional athlete was wearing t-shirts and sweats or training shorts most of the time. My game-day suits were the exception to my ultra-casual wardrobe.

Unpacking only took about twenty minutes since I kept my belongings in the contents of two suitcases most of my life. Even after three years in my last apartment in Anaheim, I never quite settled in. I spent too much time on the move to grow attached to material things. It was easy to only keep the essentials. All of my photos, books, and entertainment were on my iPad, and any memorabilia I wanted to keep was sent home to my parent's house in Toronto. Mom and Dad loved filling the living room with my jerseys, team photos, and whatever else might be necessary to remind their friends that their son was, in fact, a hockey player.

Mitch walked by as I was searching for an outlet for my phone charger. "Where are your bags?"

"In the closet," I replied and bent over to plug my charger in next to the right nightstand.

"You're not going to unpack?" He leaned against the doorframe.

"I already did." I straightened and followed his gaze around the room. The only sign I'd moved in was the pair of shoes I'd kicked off in the corner.

"Really?" he asked dubiously.

I moved to the drawers and opened a few, letting him see my stacks of folded t-shirts, socks, and sweats, then moved to the closet and opened it to show the rest of my clothes and suitcases stored on the high shelves.

"Huh." He shrugged. "Is the rest of your stuff coming later?"

"No, this is it." I was starting to get annoyed. Why wasn't this enough? I had exactly what I needed.

"You don't have a couch or a TV or"—he looked at the walls— "a poster?"

"Nope." I sat down on the end of the bed.

I seemed to have broken his brain. He stared at the floors, silent, for several moments. "Was your last place furnished?"

"They always are. All I need to bring is myself and my clothes."

His brows rose. "You're not a rookie."

"That's correct."

"I don't get it. Don't you have plates or a blanket? Anything?"

I started laughing. "Mitch, really. This is it. I'm pretty simple."

"Sorry, I'm just surprised. I should be more like you. I'm too sentimental and have a hard time getting rid of anything."

I smiled. "That's something I've never been accused of."

He chuckled. "I bet not. If you want, we can head over to the arena early and I'll give you a tour before practice."

"That would be great. Coach Romney said he wanted me there a few minutes before practice so we can talk."

"Good. I'll just grab my bag."

He left, and I pulled my duffle out from under the bed. I'd likely be getting a new one today along with Fury gear, so I only checked that I had my preferred lifting shoes and a change of clothes for after.

Mitch had changed out of his questionable sweats into a fresh pair of black training pants and matching zip-up. His maroon and black duffle was over his shoulder and he held up his keys as I walked up. "I'll drive. We can move your car to the garage afterward."

"Thanks." I forgot that it was on the other end of the block where I started this adventure.

On the short drive over, he pointed out a few key points

of interest like his favorite coffee shop, the best smoothie place, a local clothing shop that will ask for my autograph to add to their wall in exchange for a discount, and the apartment buildings of the other players.

Little of it meant much to me at the moment, but he didn't seem like the type to get annoyed with repeating himself.

As soon as we turned a corner and the arena came into view, a wave of anticipation washed over me. This was it. My new home.

I'd been on three teams since getting drafted at nineteen, and each time I was surprised by how easy it was for me to accept the change. Some guys hated getting traded and threw fits at the mention of it. I was not one of those guys.

I wanted to be where I was wanted, with a team that believed in me and a coach that saw something special enough to fight for me to join their organization.

Coach Romney had done that. He flew out to meet with me and explained where he saw me fitting in on the team and what strengths I had that the team currently lacked-- speed and a touch of fearlessness. That was all I needed to feel good about signing my new contract and driving almost seven hundred miles to a new city. I had something to contribute. The Fury was a more mature team than most in the league. They were loyal to their core players and rotated out the rest as needed. That intimidated most guys. Since I wasn't looking to settle down, it didn't bother me.

I signed a three-year contract, and beyond that, I'd stay as long as they needed me, then move on to the next team. Simple as that.

"Hey, Ralph." Mitch waved to the guard as he pulled into the parking garage under the arena for team members and employees.

As soon as we got out, Mitch paused. "You ready, Garrison? Nothing to be nervous about."

"I'm good."

"Right. Calm and collected." He gestured toward the elevator. "Let's do this."

I shook my head as I followed him. I was pretty sure he was more nervous than I was, but I appreciated his help too much to point that out.

3

VIVIAN

"Don't forget to tell Simon our six o'clock meeting is canceled. Also, I need you to order lunch for the board meeting on Friday," Jonathan, my boss, told me as he breezed by my desk on the way to his office. I didn't bother responding since he was never around long enough to hear. He was always in a rush, even halfway through the afternoon when the day was winding down. When I first started, I was always on edge and felt like I could never relax in case another request popped into his mind, but I'd learned to accept his restless nature and not take it as a personal offense.

As soon as the door shut, I picked up my phone and dialed Kerry's extension. "Hey, Viv."

"Hi, Jonathan canceled the meeting this afternoon. Did Simon get notified?"

"Let me check." I could hear clicking in the background. "I don't see any notifications, and the meeting is still on his calendar."

I wasn't surprised. I wasn't aware it had been cancelled, but there was no point in telling Jonathan that. He'd deny it like he always did. I swear he somehow expected me to read his mind. He made it seem like half the things he asked me to do were reminders of things that had already been done, but they never were.

"I'll cancel it now." I opened Jonathan's schedule and cleared out the meeting. "Oh, and send over Simon's order for lunch on Friday. We're doing sushi this time."

"Yuck," she whispered.

"I'll get you a chicken bowl or something." One of the benefits of being the assistants to the powers that be was getting to order our own lunches or breakfasts anytime there were meetings like this. The only unfortunate part was that we rarely chose where the food came from.

"Thanks." She sighed. "Has Jonathan been in a mood today?"

"He's been distracted, but no crankier than any other day. Why?"

"Simon has slammed his door three times since he got here and yelled at poor Marshy for sending in her report this morning instead of last night, even though it's technically not due until the end of the day today."

That wasn't all that unusual. Simon was over operations while Jonathan focused on the development side of things. As long as the teams were hitting their deadlines and the products were up to his standards, things were good. Simon had to deal with the daily problems that popped up and took him away from working on big projects, or more likely meeting with other rich men to discuss how successful they were.

At least, that's what it seemed like he did most of the time from what Kerry told me.

"I wonder if something HR related happened," I guessed. With a company of over two hundred people, it was a nearly daily occurrence for complaints to be filed, and those that needed to be escalated were discussed with Simon. He hated the drama, but it was a necessity that came with the job.

"Did you hear anything?" she asked.

"No, but we're always the last to know." It was a blessing and a curse, being the assistants to the head bosses. No one shared anything with us since they thought we might tell, plus we were physically separated from the rest of the employees due to our desk locations.

Kerry and I sat on opposite corners of the top floor in the building, about twenty or so yards away so each man could have a fancy corner office with a view. Between us were rows of small and medium meeting rooms as well as the central conference room that was large enough to fit the whole company at one time. That meant that unless people were walking by on their way to a meeting, we didn't see our coworkers.

She missed the socialization more than I did. I liked being isolated from distractions while still having the freedom to wander around under the pretense of running errands for Jonathan. The central gossip hub was the kitchen on the far side of this floor where most people hung out while grabbing snacks and refilling their drinks. That was usually when I overheard the latest office drama.

"I'm going to get another coffee and see if I can get any details," Kerry said. I could picture her already standing, anxious to hear the gossip.

"Okay, let me know." I hung up the phone just as my cell lit up. Jessica's name stared back at me.

She rarely called me, and never during work hours, so I hurried to pick it up.

"Hello?"

"Viv? Oh, thank heaven. I wasn't sure I'd catch you." She sounded out of breath which made me even more concerned.

"Are you okay?"

"No, I'm really not. We've got this event tonight for the mayor that starts at eight, and the whole set-up team is missing. I've called the rental company about thirty times and can't get ahold of anyone. We have twenty-five tables to set up plus decorations and the food tables, and no one to help us set up."

I glanced at the clock. It was almost four, so I wouldn't be off for another hour. I wasn't sure what I could do to help.

"Dani is calling Lance and asking for as many guys from the team who can to help, but we need all hands on deck. I hate to ask, but I'm so desperate. Is there any way you could get to the hotel down the hill from the capitol building anytime soon?"

I pulled up Jonathan's calendar. Since he canceled his meeting with Simon, he was open for the rest of the afternoon, and I didn't have anything left that needed to be done today. "I'll ask." I rarely asked for favors or time off, so I hoped Jonathan would be understanding.

"Oh, thank you! I will owe you big time."

"If I can't leave right now, I'll be off in an hour and head over then. I'll text you to let you know."

"You're the best."

I ended the call and stood, tugging down my pencil skirt. The stretchy cotton material always rode up when I wore it with tights, but it was too cold to go without right now. The compression shapewear I wore under those layers made sure all my bumps and curves stayed in place.

I knocked on Jonathan's door.

"Yes?" He called.

I peeked in and waited while he finished typing. I studied him, trying to gauge his mood. His normally smooth hair looked like he'd been running his hands through it all day and his face was pinched in concentration, but he didn't seem upset like Simon so maybe I'd get lucky.

"My roommate has an emergency and called me for help. Would it be okay if I left a bit early today?"

He tore his eyes from the laptop screen and blinked at me. "Did you finish updating the progress reports?"

I nodded. "Yeah, they're saved in your drive."

"Good, good." He looked back at his screen, "Yeah, go take care of whatever you need to. Hopefully, she's alright."

I smiled. "Thank you. Have a good evening." I shut the door quietly and hurried to gather my bag and coat. It wasn't a total surprise that he let me go without issue since I rarely asked for time off, and he was much more laid back than Simon, but I wanted to get out of the office before he remembered something he wanted me to do.

On the way to the elevators, I ran into Kerry and told her where I was going.

"Do you need my car?" she asked.

I blew out a breath. I forgot about how I was going to get to the hotel. It was on the opposite side of downtown. I could take the train, but it would require switching lines a few times and hoping I timed it right, otherwise it could take over an hour to get there. But I wasn't sure when I'd be done, and I didn't want to leave Kerry stranded.

"No, I'll order a ride." I pulled my phone out and opened the rarely-used app I saved for emergencies and special occasions.

"Ok, good luck. See you tomorrow."

I waved and stepped onto the elevator just as I got matched with a nearby car. The drive was only ten minutes, and when I followed Jess's instructions on where to find the ballroom, I was met with a bearhug.

"Thank you. Thank you!" She squeezed tightly before letting me go.

"You're welcome." I chuckled as I pulled off my coat. "What needs to be done?"

She took my things and set them against the wall with her own. "We just got the linens delivered, but nothing's been set up yet so we have to start there."

I looked over her jeans, sneakers, and messy bun and realized I was overdressed for this. I took off my cardigan, leaving me in a satin shirt, so I was less restricted and unzipped my heeled boots. This was as good as it was going to get.

"Let's get going," I said before following her to where the rows of chairs and tables waited. So far, only three round tables were set up. We rolled another table to its designated spot and pulled out the legs, counting to three together before flipping it to stand up.

"Perfect. Only twenty-one left."

"Where's Dani? And the other backup?" I asked while rolling the next table.

"Dani's helping the caterers set up, and hopefully backup gets here soon." Jess blew a loose hair from her face.

We'd set up another two tables when the doors swung open.

"The cavalry has arrived!" Lance bellowed.

Mikey followed behind with Jake and Jason. I'd met them a few times at Jess and Dani's office when Lance had invited them over, along with Jason's fiancé, Taylor. The three couples were relatively new so they seemed to have formed a mini group within the team. I'd noticed from the handful of games Jess invited me to that there was a hierarchy among the wives and girlfriends of the players. They were known as the Pride and consisted of the beautiful, modelesque women that were only intimidating until you got to know them. So far, they'd been perfectly nice to me. Jess was nervous about being accepted, but I could tell they liked her.

Another two men walked in that I didn't recognize. One was nearly as wide as he was tall with a glorious red beard and thick head of disheveled hair that seemed to float around him like a flame. The other was much slimmer and a few inches shorter. He had short brown hair and a long well-trimmed beard. He was much leaner than his companion, but still had the signature muscles in his arms and legs of all the other players. Mikey passed me, and I touched his arm.

"Who are they?" I tilted my head in the direction of the newcomers.

He twisted to see, then smiled. "Like what you see?"

I narrowed my eyes. "That's not what I meant. I just don't think I've seen them before."

"Well, the enormous one with red hair is Mitch Doranon, or Dory, as we call him."

I chuckled at the nickname. The brute looked like he belonged in the highland games throwing logs across fields. How had I ever missed him on the ice?

"The other guy, with the holy grail of beards, is brand new. Just arrived this week. His name's Garrison." Mikey paused. "I forgot his first name. Porter? Peter?"

"Parker," Jake said casually as he walked by.

"Yeah! That's it. Parker Garrison." Mikey clapped me on the shoulder and followed Jake to the tables that needed to be set up.

Parker Garrison was already at work, setting up chairs with Dory. He was significantly smaller than his teammate, but I was pretty sure everyone looked tiny next to Dory. Parker had short dark hair and deep olive skin with broad shoulders. I stared at his arms, bulging under the strain of carrying several chairs at the same time, then forced myself to look away and get back to work.

I rotated between tables and chairs until everything was

set up. Jess dumped an armful of white tablecloths against my chest and moved to the other side of the room.

"Here, I'll help you." Dory stood next to me with his arms out expectantly. I handed him one and sat the rest on the closest table.

"Thank you." I grinned up at him, and we took opposite ends of the linen and draped it over the table before going around and tucking it in front of the chairs.

"I haven't seen you around before," he said. "Which one of the blokes do you belong to?"

I paused and stared. There were multiple things wrong with his statement, the first being his wording. "I don't *belong* to anyone."

He threw his hands up. "That's not what I meant. I just was making a joke." He rubbed his long beard. "I'm sorry. Bad taste. I'm a feminist, I swear."

I pursed my lips, not believing a word of it.

"I'm digging myself in deeper, aren't I?" The apples of his cheeks, the only part of his face besides his nose that wasn't covered by ginger hair, were red.

I finally let out a laugh. "I was going to go easy on you because of the whole Dory thing, but I can see you'll need my mercy for your slips up."

He dropped his head and groaned. "Who told you?"

"Mikey," I admitted.

He searched the room until he caught sight of him. "I'll get back at him." He met my eyes again, and his shoulders slumped. "Fine, you can call me Dory, if you forget about my blunder."

I pretended to consider it before agreeing.

"And now that you know my name, may I ask yours?"

"Vivian, and I'm not affiliated with any of your team-mates. I'm Jess's roommate, and she called for extra help."

He paused. "So, you're single?"

I turned to hide my warming cheeks and picked up another table cloth. I wasn't positive, but there was a strong probability he was flirting with me. While I wasn't sure I was into the Scottish lumberjack-type, it was still flattering.

"I am." I flung the tablecloth out so he could catch the other side, and we brought it down together.

"Interesting." He kept his eyes down.

"Is it?"

Finally, he looked up. "Yes, I was just telling the new guy that all the pretty girls in the city were taken by our teammates, but here I am, being proven wrong. There's hope yet."

"You flatter me, sir." I raised a brow. "Or are you still trying to make up for your previous comment."

"Never." He acted affronted.

"Good because a few pretty words aren't going to win me over."

"But it works for them." He nodded back where the rest of the guys were.

"Well, they have a pretty face to back it up."

He let out a boisterous laugh that echoed through the nearly empty room. I glanced around, feeling eyes on us.

"Shh. They're staring," I whispered and scowled at him.

He cringed and ducked his head, but didn't stop laughing. "Sorry, but that was an exceptional burn."

I thought over my words and realized what I said and how insulting it could have been. "Oh no!" I stepped toward him. "That's not what I meant. I don't mean that you don't have a pretty face too."

He was still chuckling when he waved his hand. "Looks like we both know how to stick our feet in our mouths."

4

PARKER

The laughter from the far side of the room caught my attention a few times, but I tried not to stare. Mitch, or Dory as I was told to call him by the other guys, was helping a woman I hadn't been introduced to. Lance and Jake pointed out Jess and Dani when we walked in but neither of them said anything about her.

"Tug it a little bit more to your side," Mikey directed.

I focused on the tablecloth and centered it before we let it fall. "Do you know who that is?"

Mikey walked around the table, tucking in the linen as we were instructed, and glanced around. "Who?"

"The woman talking to Dory." I signaled in their direction.

He spun around, gaining their attention, and waved. Great. I should have specified being discreet, though I wasn't sure Mikey knew what that meant. He was as blunt and direct as they came.

"Oh, that's Jess's roommate." He walked to the next table and unfolded the cloth, handing me one side. "She probably got called in to help too."

I tucked away that knowledge while we continued to work our way around the room, but it was hard not to get pulled back in her direction. Their laughing was near-constant with random jumps in volume.

"At least some of us are having a good time," Mikey groaned. "I was planning on taking an ice bath and relaxing tonight."

"We need to move, people!" Dani started clapping her hands. "I want to see some hustle."

Jake shook his head and moved a bit faster around his table, tucking as he went.

"She does remember we're free labor, right?" Mikey muttered only loud enough for me to hear.

I still wasn't sure how I'd been roped into this. I was heading out of the locker room with Mitch when Jake stopped us and asked for help. Since Mitch was my ride, I was forced along. It wasn't like I had any plans for the evening, though. Plus, this showed I was a team player. Hopefully, word would get back to the coaches or captains.

"New guy," Dani called, and I looked up, assuming I was the only new person she didn't know the name of.

"Yeah?" I stepped back so we could cover our next table.

She made her way over and eyed me. "Thanks for coming. I appreciate the extra hands."

"Sure." I didn't mention that it wasn't necessarily by choice. "Anytime."

"I'm ordering in food. Do you have any pizza topping preferences?"

Ordering food was always a tricky situation when you're around new people. Do you go the honest route and admit what you like, or try to be easy-going and low-maintenance?

"I like either a meat combo or meat and veggie combo." I didn't add that I'd pick off the mushrooms of anything that came near my plate.

"Great. You, Lance, and Dory can share one." She turned to Mikey. "I'm getting a pepperoni with extra peppers and onions for you."

"Thanks, Dani." He winked before she moved on.

"I guess that means we're here for a bit," I mentioned.

He groaned. "At least she has the sense to feed us."

By the time the pizza was delivered, all of the tables and chairs were arranged and covered, and Jess and her roommate were putting fancy glass centerpieces on each. The event was set to begin in an hour, and to me, the ballroom appeared ready, but Dani stopped us from eating to have us move the banquet tables three feet across to be better centered in the room.

"Perfect." She nodded as she slowly turned and scanned the room for anything out of place.

"Everything's done," Jess confirmed. "It's time to let the caterers take over."

Dani let out a small sigh. "Okay, yeah. You're right."

"Let's go." Jess picked up half of the boxes, and Lance helped with the other half. "We can eat in this room."

She led us into a conference meeting room with a large enough table to accommodate us. Mikey dropped a short stack of paper plates and napkins onto the table, then started lifting lids so the pizzas were in a line on one end of the table. Jason and Jake handed out plates to the rest of us.

"Thanks for dinner, Dani. You didn't have to. We're happy to help," Mitch said while loading his plate.

"We really, really appreciate you guys coming in. There was no way we could have finished in time without you." She turned to her roommate. "And thank you, Viv. I know you had to leave work early. We owe you."

So, Viv was her name. I eyed her. She didn't look like a Viv. In my mind, that was someone that wore turtlenecks and fitted pantsuits, with tightly pulled-back hair. She had long, straight brown hair the color of dark caramel that hung loosely around her shoulders, and she wore a shiny, green shirt with a pencil skirt that hugged her plentiful curves. She was shorter than Jess and Dani and might have been easily overlooked in comparison, but her bright smile and the constant ring of laughter I'd listened to before kept drawing me in.

"Don't mention it. I'm happy I could help." She sounded genuine.

"Next spa day is on me," Jess promised her.

It was my turn to grab a plate, so I took a few slices and found a seat next to Mitch.

"Mind if I sit?" Viv asked from Mitch's other side.

"Not at all." He grinned up at her. "I was saving it for you."

"Well, thank you, sir." She glanced over at me. "Sorry I didn't get a chance to meet you earlier. I'm Vivian."

I offered a small wave. "Parker."

"He's new to the team. Just arrived this week," Mitch started.

"And how do you like things so far?" she asked, locking eyes on me.

"Seems nice." I shrugged. "I haven't had a chance to see anything other than the arena."

"Hopefully you get a chance to settle in soon, but it must be hard to move in the middle of the season."

"It's part of the job." I didn't want any of the other guys hearing and thinking I wasn't happy to be here, so I added. "The Fury is a great team though."

"I got traded midseason back in my early years," Jason jumped in front from the other side of the table. "It was jarring at first, but I kind of like being thrown into the mix and being forced to adapt. When you're traded before the season, you have time to overthink and psych yourself out."

"That's true," I agreed. "Arriving and immediately going

to practice and having a game tomorrow hasn't given me any time to do anything but focus on the game."

"Have they been nice to you?" Viv asked.

I looked around at the guys all watching me and let out a small laugh. "Yes?"

"You can be honest," she said, eyeing them.

"Yeah, one word, and we'll take care of them," Jess said, in what I assumed was her attempt at a threatening voice.

"Well, we can pass word onto Chloe, and she'll take care of them," Dani said with a chuckle.

Ah. That was a name I recognized. She was not only the woman from the front office that helped coordinate my move, but I learned she was the wife of one of the alternative captains and the sister of the other. Her sister-in-law was the daughter of Coach Romney, and she was the ringleader of the Pride, the group of wives and girlfriends of the players that came to each game and acted as the spirit squad. Mitch pointed them out to me during practice. Overall, she was the most connected person I'd ever met. I had no doubt if I had an issue with one of my teammates, she would be the one to take care of it.

"Don't threaten us like that." Mikey shivered.

"She only uses her power for good," Dani reassured me before glaring at Mikey. "If you didn't get yourself into trouble, you wouldn't have to fear her."

"I was having a bad time," he grunted. I wanted to know what he was talking about, but stayed quiet.

"So?" Viv watched me curiously. "Are they?"

I nodded, "Yeah, they've been great. Very welcoming."

Lance snorted. "Good answer."

"Hey," she snapped at him. "Be kind, or the party is canceled."

He narrowed his eyes at her, but she didn't back down. "Fine."

Party? I glanced at Mitch, and he shrugged. So, he wasn't invited either.

"Oh, Dory! You and Parker are invited to our place on Friday for a dinner party," Jess grinned.

"Why am I just hearing about this?" Mitch turned his eyes on Lance.

"Calm down. It's not a big deal. I was going to mention it tomorrow." Lance waved him off.

"Yeah, we're trying to keep it quiet. It's the first time we're hosting, and we wanted to keep it pretty small," Mikey added.

"Why?" Jake asked.

"It's always Chloe or Emma or Madi that host, and we rarely get invited. I get it, we're the newer guys, younger, and they've all gotten married and started having babies. I don't think they mean to do it, but they have their group, and I get that, but I don't want to sit on the sidelines forever," Lance admitted. "This is like a practice to see how things go, and eventually we can invite more and more people."

This was key information for me. There was a divide on the team, at least off the ice. The vets versus the rookies, or at least the younger guys. Where did that leave me if Lance had been on the team for a few years? Was I lucky to even be here, eating pizza with these guys? Mitch would have to catch me up later.

"Whoa, I wasn't aware that was the plan," Viv said glancing from Jess to Lance.

"It won't always be at your place," he cajoled, but she didn't look like she believed him behind her narrowed eyes.

"Then where?" she challenged.

He looked around the table, pausing on Dani and Jake. "Maybe?"

"Nope," Dani cut him off. "You've seen our layout. It's

perfect for two or three couples, but anything more, and it's way too cramped."

"Jason?" Lance caught him with a slight raise to his mouth.

His eyes darted around. "What?"

"Has Taylor ever mentioned wanting to host a dinner party?" he asked.

Jason shook his head. "She pretty much works and plans our wedding. I don't think she has the mental capacity for anything else right now."

Lance shrugged. "Then I guess this plan is destined to fail. We'll remain the outcasts forever."

Jess rolled her eyes. "It's not a popularity contest. Some of the guys are just at different places in their lives. That's fine."

Mikey and Lance shared a look.

"What is it?" Dani sighed. "Do you feel like that? An outsider?" She directed the question to Jason.

He shrugged. "I guess. It wasn't really until Taylor came back in the picture that any of the veterans or the Pride cared about me."

"And that's because the women got involved," Lance pointed out.

"Yeah," Jason admitted. "They do tend to insert themselves in our personal lives."

Dani and Jess shared a grin. I glanced at Viv, but she was focused on picking onions off her pizza. Was she included in that group?

"So, get yourself a girlfriend, and the team will accept you as one of their own." Jake smiled at Dani.

"That's true. The Pride is more powerful than any of you could ever wish to be," Dani remarked.

"I have one!" Lance pointed at Jess who leaned back to avoid getting hit in the face.

"And I'm good friends with them. Thanks for that." She winked and took a big bite of her pizza.

"But I'm still treated like a peripheral player," Lance complained.

"Maybe that's a problem that can only be fixed on the ice," Jake pointed out.

Lance glared. "What's that supposed to mean?"

Jake shrugged.

I watched them like it was a tennis match, hitting words back and forth. This was a part of the team dynamic that would take time to understand. I didn't want to be too nosy when this sounded like a personal problem with Lance.

"Murray and Schultz and Hartman care about what you do during a game. You'll earn their respect there, not at some dinner party," Jason said.

"That's true," Mitch said with a nod.

"What are you talking about?" Lance asked him. "You've never been to one of their parties."

He rubbed his beard. "Doesn't mean I've never been invited."

Lance leaned forward. "What do you mean?"

"I get an email or text about them occasionally, but I just don't like socializing with the team on my time off," Mitch explained while Lance looked like his head was going to explode.

"Why not?"

"I'm with you all nearly every day. We practice, train, travel, and have games that take up most of my life. Why would I want to be around you even more? I go to team events and birthdays, but anything nonessential, I sit out."

Jason agreed. "That's how I felt before Taylor."

Lance huffed and leaned back.

"Don't pout. We'll help you make friends." Jess patted his shoulder.

"You can use our apartment as much as you need," Viv said with a touch of humor in her voice. "We don't want you left out of the sandbox with the cool kids."

Lance glared at her, and Mikey poked him in the ribs with his elbow.

"Thanks," he finally choked out.

"Oh. We've got to go," Dani said to Jess. She checked her phone and jumped up.

"Thanks again, you guys!" Jess waved as they rushed out of the room.

This whole conversation was bizarre, but I learned more about the inner workings of the team in one meal than I would have in months of practice. I just wasn't sure where I wanted to fit in.

5

VIVIAN

They hadn't lied. Lance and Mikey really had taken care of everything for the dinner party. When I got home after work on Friday, the furniture was rearranged so there was a more open area in the center of our apartment. I wasn't sure what that was supposed to accomplish, but this wasn't my deal.

"Hey, people are supposed to start arriving in an hour. Where's the food?" Mikey asked Lance as I tried to slide behind him to the hallway that led to my room.

He almost stepped on me, but I put my hand on his shoulder and he moved.

"It's supposed to be here by now. I'll call," Lance replied.

When I passed Jess's room, she called out my name.

"How bad is it?" She leaned forward out of the doorway but there was nothing to see.

I shrugged. "No food yet, I guess."

She rolled her eyes. "They won't let me do anything. They said they wanted to take care of everything."

"That would explain the sitting situation." I giggled.

Her eyes widened. "Oh no. What did they do?"

"All the chairs and couches are pushed against the walls so there's just this huge empty space."

"Are they planning on having dancing?" She joked, then froze. "Please tell me they aren't actually planning on having dancing."

"That's not a horrible guess, but you'll have to ask them." I wasn't qualified to interpret their actions.

"I'll have to make it very clear I had nothing to do with this. I don't want anyone thinking Dani or I helped them."

"I'm sure it will be fine." I could only say that because, one, it didn't affect me unless something was broken. And two, this wasn't a public event or anything that would be documented. It was just some friends getting together for dinner.

"You're right." She sighed. "As long as everyone has fun, it's a success."

"Is it only couples coming?"

"No, Mikey is single, and he didn't invite anyone. Plus, Dory and Parker are coming now." She hesitated. "You might be the only single lady, though."

I almost asked if I could invite Kerry, but I was already a fringe participant. I likely wouldn't have been invited if it wasn't taking place at my apartment.

"That's okay. I think Dory and I are friends now." We clicked once we got each other laughing. He was an easy person to be around, and Parker seemed nice enough, if not a little shy. We could form a singles alliance with Mikey.

She tossed her head back, laughing. "I noticed that. He's the silent, brooding one on the team. I think I've only heard him speak three times, yet you had him laughing and smiling all night." She wagged her brows. "Is there anything I should know about?"

I shook my head. "Not at all."

It was surprising to hear Dory was quiet around Jess. It

had taken a few minutes to stumble through the awkward start to our conversation, but he loosened up quickly enough. Maybe Jess just hadn't tried very hard.

"It wouldn't be the worst thing." She grinned like a woman with a scheme brewing. "You could start dating, then you'd be officially a part of the Pride."

I did envy her instant friend group, but that didn't mean I wanted to date Dory for his connections.

"I think there's strong friendship potential there." I hoped she would drop it. If I was okay with the situation, she should be too.

"Fine, but that doesn't mean I'm giving up. There are a few other single guys on the team." She paused. "Oh, like the new guy."

Parker. Mister tall, dark, and handsome was someone I could see myself crushing on, but I stopped those thoughts the night we met before anything could happen. There was no use getting excited only to get let down later.

He didn't seem interested in me at all, and I wasn't going to fight that. I just accepted the truth and moved on.

"I don't think so." I stepped back out of her room. "I've got to get ready."

Her shoulders slumped, but she didn't argue.

The doorbell rang a moment after I closed my bedroom door behind me. Hopefully, that was the food so Lance and Mikey could calm down. It might just be a silly dinner party, but it was important to them, and I wanted it to be successful. Whatever that meant for them. I was ready to play the role they needed. If they wanted me to hang back and make sure the food and drinks stayed stocked, I'd be happy to. If they wanted me to socialize and get people involved in a game or conversation, then I'd set it up. It's what friends did for each other, and they'd made an effort to make sure I knew they considered me one of theirs.

After changing into leggings and a long, cozy sweater, I headed out to assess the situation. I expected chaos, but the aluminum catering dishes were neatly arranged on the kitchen counters with serving spoons and tongs next to each. Mikey was pulling out plastic cups to go behind the plates and utensils.

"This looks great." I noticed the quiet music. "What can I help with?"

Lance stood in the center of the room with his hands on his hips. "Do you think this is enough seating?"

Since every chair, bench, and couch in the apartment was already being used, there was only one answer. "I think it will be perfect."

I still didn't know how many people to expect, but I didn't want to ask in case they ended up disappointed later.

"She's right. You've done everything you can. Now you just have to wait." Jess put her arms around Lance's middle from behind and rested her head against his back.

I smiled at the adorable couple and walked through the kitchen, checking for anything that might have been overlooked.

"They're so gross," Mikey whispered when I was a few feet away.

I giggled. "Someone sounds jealous."

He rolled his eyes, not helping his case. "I'm happy for them and all, but it does kind of suck to be one of the last men standing. I thought we'd be the bachelors of the team forever."

I patted his back. "If you want a relationship like theirs, your time will come."

From the stories I'd heard, Lance dating Jess was a blessing for both of them. The two of them had been serial daters and only on the hunt for instant gratification. With

Lance settling down, Mikey had a choice to make. Follow in his friends' footsteps or party alone.

"Yeah, maybe." A knock sounded, and he spun around to answer the door. "Hey, guys!"

Jake and Dani walked in, followed by Jason and Taylor. Lance greeted them, and he and Mikey took their coats and put them in Jess's room as they'd planned.

Taylor met my eye and grinned. "First-class service here."

I laughed. "They're really going all out tonight."

She scanned the room and nodded. "I can tell."

I didn't know Taylor very well, but she always made sure I felt included at the games. She only moved to Salt Lake within the last year and admitted once she felt like an outsider too. She and Jason had been high school sweethearts and reconnected after running into each other in Raleigh when the Fury was playing the Sand Storms there.

I loved their story. It was so romantic and full of hope.

My favorite part of attending the games was being filled in on how the women met their players during the intermission between periods. Some of them were nearly unbelievable, like Dani and Jake falling in love while she was planning a previous player's wedding. Others were almost comical, like Kendall hating Wyatt because of her allegiance to her home team, and Chloe trying to hide her relationship from the entire team, including her twin brother who she lived with at the time.

I watched Jess while listening to each of them tell me their love stories, and I saw the dreamy look in her eyes. She wanted her story with Lance to end the same way, her very own happily ever after. I glanced over to Mikey. Maybe that was what we all wished for.

"Jason told me you helped out setting up that event the other night. I wish I'd known. I would have come over and helped too."

"Oh, it was fine. It only took about two hours, then we had pizza."

She nodded. "Still, Dani and Jess should know by now that we all step up when one of us needs it."

One of us. What would it be like to be a part of a group like that? As much as I loved Kerry and knew she would go out of her way for me, their relationships were different. They were more than friends or teammates, they were family. Taylor might not realize it yet, but she wasn't an outsider any more than Dani or Sydney or Addison was.

The door opened, and Amelia walked in with her boyfriend. I searched my brain until I remembered his name, Derek. I'd only met Amelia once since she was a team trainer and worked behind the bench during the games, but her sister Elena made sure I was introduced a few weeks ago.

"Hello, ladies!" She beamed and gave Taylor and me a brief hug. "It's so nice to be around women for once."

Taylor laughed. "Oh, your life is so hard being around all those men all day."

Amelia snorted. "Those very stinky boys that come to me hurting and therefore cranky."

I scrunched my nose. "Good point."

"Plus, it's not like I can ogle at my brother-in-law or all my friends' husbands and boyfriends."

"You better not." Derek appeared behind her and kissed her cheek.

"Hey, loser," Taylor teased.

Derek narrowed his eyes. "Aren't we passed that?"

She shook her head. "Absolutely not. I will drag this out until your dying day."

I looked between them, and Amelia sighed. "They had a competition running the steps at the arena, and Taylor beat him."

"Yes, I did." She said triumphantly. "The prize was that the winner got to call the loser by their title."

"And I didn't set a time limit," Derek grumbled.

"Fool." Amelia shook her head.

"How was I supposed to know she was some sort of sprinter?" He shook his head and walked away.

Taylor laughed. "He's still convinced I cheated. It's not my fault he doesn't train enough on cardio."

"He skates for hours every day," I said. "How much more does he need to do?"

She shrugged. "Enough to beat me."

Lance let out a whistle that ended all conversations in the room. "Thanks for coming, everyone. We're really happy to have you over." The front door opened, and Dory and Parker slid in.

All eyes went to them, and Dory held up a hand. "Sorry we're late."

Parker's face was bright red, and he ducked his head.

"Welcome!" Mikey cheered.

"As I was saying," Lance continued. "We owe a thanks to Jess and Viv for graciously hosting, and the food is ready, so let's get to eating!"

"Here, here!" Mikey threw up his fist, and the room filled with laughter.

A line formed to get plates, and Mikey and Lance were distracted, so I made my way to Dory and Parker. "Hi, guys. I can take your coats."

Dory grinned and tugged on his sleeves, slipping his off and handing it to me. "Good to see you again, Vivi."

I paused at the nickname. It wasn't what most people called me, but I didn't mind. "You too, Mitch."

His smile brightened, and I had a feeling he preferred that name.

"I can hang this up," Parker said, pulling my attention toward him.

"Okay." I turned, headed to the hall, and stepped into Jess's room. I laid Mitch's jacket on top of the bed, and Parker mirrored me with his own.

"Is this your room?" He was studying the sparse furniture and photos.

"No, this is Jess's."

He nodded. "That makes more sense. It didn't seem like you."

I paused. He thought he had an idea of what my room would look like? Intrigued, I stopped in the doorway. "What did you expect?"

He took a step back and licked his lip. "I don't know. More colorful?" I waited and he continued. "More personal."

"Jess has only lived here for about six weeks." Not that she mentioned adding anything else or redecorating. She seemed to be a minimalist, minus her nearly overflowing closet.

"Were you friends before she moved in?" he asked.

"No, my previous roommate moved out and I thought I'd like the extra space, but after a little while I decided I wanted to have someone around. I posted an ad, and she responded. She wasn't the first to call. I made sure to meet and interview the women that seemed normal then decided Jess was the best fit."

"Cool." His brows rose. "How long have you lived here?"

"Almost two years." I glanced at my door trying to remember if my room had anything embarrassing in sight. "Let's see if you were right."

I opened the door, and he followed me in. After a moment of looking around, the corner of his lip tipped up. "Yeah, this is right."

The walls were already painted a cheery yellow when I moved in, and I liked the color enough to keep it. Plus, it matched well enough with my dark coral, teal, and white bedding and decorations. It was a comfortable space. Not too sparse to notice when things were out of place, like Jess's. But not so cluttered it was overwhelming. Just, lived in.

"I like it." He smiled down at me, and a sparkle appeared in his eyes I hadn't noticed before. It changed his whole appearance from quiet and brooding to warm and friendly.

"Thanks." I turned and headed back to the party.

6

PARKER

I was surprised she let me see her room. I hadn't expected that when I initially asked about it. The room where we left the coats just didn't fit her. Well, who I thought she was. But she proved to be just as warm and welcoming as my first impression led me to believe.

Mikey directed us to get in line for food, so we joined the back behind Dani and Jake.

"Hey, Viv. I love that sweater. That shade of pink looks great on you," Dani finished, then turned to me. "Hello again."

"Hi," I replied. I never particularly considered myself shy or introverted before the trade, but it felt like everyone here had such large, imposing personalities. It was too easy to fade to the shadows.

"Thanks." Viv offered a gracious smile, but it didn't reach her eyes. Why not? The light pink really did look nice.

I had to physically stop myself from reaching out and touching the fabric. It looked incredibly soft.

We shuffled forward, and I picked up two plates, handing

the extra to Viv. The corner of her lip curved for a flash before she stared at the ground.

Something had changed between the time we left her room and now, but I had no idea what. It felt like her light, or spark, just went out.

Dani and Jake were discussing the food options, so I ducked my head to whisper, "Are you okay?"

Her eyes met mine, revealing her surprise. "Yeah?"

She wasn't even convincing herself.

I waited a moment before straightening. She had no reason to confide in me, but it bothered me far more than it should. She seemed so confident and positive. Seeing her upset felt wrong.

She cleared her throat and stepped forward. Spread before us was what looked like taco or burrito fixings. At the beginning were flour and corn tortillas next to a large bowl of lettuce, then meats, rice, beans, and various toppings.

Viv scooped lettuce onto her plate then continued on, making a delicious looking salad.

I put a flour tortilla down first then began building my burrito. By the time I was done, and had rolled it up with a side of salsa and guacamole on the plate, almost everyone was seated. There were only a few empty seats left, ones next to Derek, Jason, and Mitch.

I'd tried to call him Dory, but it didn't feel right. It was like an inside joke I wasn't a part of, and he didn't seem to necessarily love the nickname.

I wanted to go to my roommate since he felt like the safest option, but that wasn't the point of coming tonight. If I wanted to get to know him better, all I had to do was leave my bedroom. I'd encouraged him to come with me so I could get to know more of the guys outside of formal team events.

I'd spent the least amount of time with Derek, so I headed toward him. "This seat taken?"

He shook his head, and Amelia smiled at me. "Sit down. I was hoping to have a chance to get to talk to you tonight."

I sat and carefully balanced my plate on my knees while putting my water next to my feet.

"So where are you from?" she asked.

I wasn't sure what she meant, so I covered both options. "I grew up in Toronto. My last team was Anaheim."

"And you're single?" She grinned, and Derek shook his head.

"Don't answer that, Garrison. The women love a project, but nothing tops a matchmaking mission." He gave me a warning look.

"That's not true." Amelia swatted his arm.

"It's absolutely true." He lowered his fork from his mouth and pointed to Jake. "You guys meddled in his life more than should be legal."

"And look at how happy they are now!" she countered.

"You moved Taylor across the country without telling him."

"We helped her move. It was her choice."

"And Dani? You guys went overboard again and moved her from Mexico."

"She had nowhere else to go!" She waved him off. "That sounds worse than it really was," she said to me.

"They found Sydney and basically hired her without telling Brandon," Derek added.

"And now they're married!" Amelia's voice was loud enough to catch everyone's attention. She realized it and raised a brow. "I challenge someone here to give an example of when the Pride interfered and it didn't result in something positive." She leaned toward me. "They're the group of women, the wives and girlfriends. They go to practices and the games."

I nodded. Even though I'd already been told about them, I appreciated her making sure I was clued in.

"They're everywhere." Jason shuddered.

A few people laughed, but no one else spoke.

"See, nothing bad," Amelia challenged Derek.

"It's true. I wouldn't have my business, or Jake, if it wasn't for you guys." Dani grinned, and Jake kissed the top of her head.

"Which means I wouldn't have my job or my man either." Jess leaned into Lance, who looked pleased.

"Same!" Amelia pointed at Derek. "I wouldn't live here or have my job or you without the Pride."

I looked at Mikey and Mitch across from me. "What about you guys?"

"Oh, I try to stay out of the way," Mitch said with wide eyes, like I might have just put a mark on him.

"They're not my biggest fan," Mikey admitted.

"Why not?" Again, the words were out before I could think better of it, but this was the worst part of being the new guy. There was so much history that you didn't know. The best way to find out was to ask.

"I went through a rough patch," he said to his plate. When he didn't continue, I glanced around, but the guys avoided my eyes. This wasn't a topic for tonight apparently.

"Any who." Taylor sliced through the tension. "What are some things you're into?"

I glanced to Derek, who wasn't paying attention, before looking back at her. "Like hobbies?"

She nodded. "Yeah, what do you do outside of practice?"

"And games and travel and promos and photoshoots?" I expected a question like this from a fan but not a team employee, especially not one that's so immersed with the private lives of the players. She had to know we had so very little time outside of the team for anything else.

She waited, but I didn't know what to say. There wasn't time growing up for other interests. It was school, homework, practice, and traveling. I didn't learn to play an instrument or draw or even get into video games. I liked music as much as the next person, but I wasn't really dedicated to any single artist or even genre. I watched movies as a way to pass time on planes, and the last book I read was during my senior year of high school.

The last thing I expected tonight was to have an existential crisis in the middle of some near-strangers' living room.

"Did you hang out with your teammates a lot?" she tried.

I shrugged. "Yeah, I guess."

My Anaheim team was younger than the Fury, so most of us were single, but that didn't mean we took weekend trips together or went to Disneyland on a free afternoon.

She tilted her head. "Hockey's your whole life, isn't it?"

It wasn't meant to be an insult. I could see her genuine curiosity, but I suddenly felt self-conscious.

Wasn't that how it was meant to be for us? Our jobs were playing. We didn't have regular nine-to-five hours and weekends off. During the offseason, we had the chance to travel and head home, but I generally stuck around and trained. I wasn't enough of a superstar to think I could take three months off. I had to stay on top of my game. Be my very best in order to hold my position in the NHL and not drop into the American League.

"That's okay." She offered a smile. "We, the Pride, try to plan things to get you guys out of your heads and to give you the chance to take a break. Even if it's just for a night. You're always invited."

Derek huffed. "Don't think that's something everyone gets offered either."

She nudged him. "Don't listen to him. He had a rough patch too, but you get the energy you put out. He was prickly and arrogant, so it's not hard to imagine why the guys weren't so interested in spending time together away from the arena."

I nearly coughed out the food in my mouth. That was shocking to hear from her.

"It's all in the past now." She patted his knee. "Ultimately, it's up to you. If you want to be included, you're welcome, but if you prefer to have a separation between work and your personal life, that's fine too."

She stood, walking toward the kitchen. I let out a sigh, thinking I was done with this conversation, but Derek leaned closer.

"That's not entirely true. Remember what I said before. Those women will take one look at you and see a project to work on. They don't think anyone can be happy alone." He huffed, "Some of the guys are just as bad. They don't take you seriously unless you're in a committed relationship."

I didn't like the sound of that, but if Derek and Mikey both had negative experiences in the past while they were single, maybe that's what the team thought was the problem. A woman in your life made you stable or something.

It was too soon to know for sure if his theory was right. I'd only been on the team for a few days, but I could tell that there was a tight group of the core guys. Legends, actually. One of the major reasons I was so unaffected by the trade was that I was going to one of the best teams in the league. The repeat champions. I wanted to be a part of this elite group.

But did I want in further? Was being their teammate enough?

I watched the couples and thought of the women that appeared at each practice. Was I ready for that? For commitment and settling down? I wasn't anything close to a partier or player or womanizer. The reason I'd lasted this long was by keeping my head down and working hard. That didn't seem to be enough for this team. They wanted a family. They wanted me to be more than an asset on the ice.

If Derek's advice could be trusted, I didn't want to ask for their help finding someone. That would grow out of my control too quickly, and I didn't want anyone thinking my mind was on dating instead of playing. But it wasn't like I could pull a girlfriend out of thin air. I didn't know anyone in the city except the people in this room.

A laugh hit my ears, and I searched for the source. There, Viv had her head tossed back and her hand on Taylor's arm. Jason was grinning, and Taylor was wiping her eyes. Why was she always at the center of the entertainment? From what I gathered, she was an outsider. Not truly a part of the Pride, but they still seemed to include her. Lance and Mikey talked about her like they were all friends.

Maybe she could help me. Everyone liked her, and she was close enough to the inner circle without actually being one of the obsessive Pride women. She could help me find my place here and with the Fury.

Mitch walked up behind her and rubbed her shoulders. She tilted her head up and smiled. Was he interested in her? Did she like him? They seemed to hit it off the other night. I'd have to bring it up with him later or find a different option. But why did that suddenly sound terrible? I didn't really know her, but watching her interact with Mitch, how easily they spoke and teased and laughed, made me feel ... jealous? No that couldn't be right. Excluded.

Maybe I was jealous they formed a bond so quickly, and I tend to struggle to make friends that quickly with anyone. It didn't mean I was necessarily jealous of him because it was Viv. *Right?*

7

VIVIAN

"Hey, how was your weekend?" Kerry bumped my shoulder while I stared at the coffee maker, willing it to go faster. Jonathan was already in his office and had a meeting starting in less than ten minutes I had to attend to take notes. I needed to get this caffeine in my system and get the agenda pulled up on my tablet with the comments Jonathan added the night before.

"It was fine." I rocked the bottle of creamer back and forth. "The party was fun, and the guys did clean up as they promised."

"Nice." She tapped her nails on the counter.

"How was your date?" She texted me on Saturday night to tell me she had more to share.

"Oh, it was so great. I really like him, Viv."

I caught her grin out of the corner of my eye and turned to her. "That's great. Where did you guys go?"

"We got dinner at Modesto and saw the symphony. It was really lovely." She sighed. "Then he kissed me before saying goodnight."

I raised a brow. She usually stuck to her "no kissing on the first date" rule. He had to be something special for her to break it. "So, when are you seeing him again?"

"Friday." She reached out and moved my full mug toward me and put hers in its place. "He has tickets to the hockey game."

"That will be fun."

Her eyes widened. "You should see if you can get tickets with Jess, then we'll arrange an accidental run-in so you can meet him."

I finished making my drink and headed out of the kitchen. "I will definitely ask her."

Chugging down my coffee wasn't an option when it was still so hot, but I drank as much as I could manage while grabbing my tablet from my desk and finding the meeting room we were using. No one else was there yet, so I made sure it was tidy and stocked with the correct cords for Jonathan's computer and markers for the whiteboard that took up an entire wall.

I settled into a chair in the corner as the various project managers trickled in. At nine on the dot, Jonathan strode in and began the meeting.

For once, everyone took their own notes for the changes and tasks they'd been assigned, so when I sent the follow up email, they wouldn't be shocked. I also had to speak up once to remind Jonathan of a minor change he'd mentioned in one of his comments.

My tablet was linked to my account that also connected my phone and laptop so I could get any necessary messages and emails no matter where I was. Most of the time, I ignored anything personal that came through while I was in meetings, but this wasn't one that required much of my mental space, so when Kerry sent me a text to remind me to ask Jess, I decided to get it over with now so I could tell her it was done. We were both the type to have a running to-do list, and this would sit on both of ours until I confirmed I was going to the game.

I quietly tapped out a message asking Jess, then told Kerry it was done and I'd let her know when I had a response.

She replied with the profile picture of the guy from her date, AJ. He was average-looking, thin with a decent amount of mousy brown hair. He had kind eyes and looked like he would be kind and respectful. Just want every woman wanted. Looks faded, but if he was sweet and lit her up, then I was now his cheerleader.

I told her he was a catch and switched back to the agenda. One of the managers wrote me a note in the margins, asking me to schedule a follow-up meeting for everyone in a week, so I went to the company calendar and created the event, and sent out the invitations.

Jess replied, so I went back to the messages. She already had a ticket waiting for me and recommended I invest in some Fury gear soon since this was going to be a regular thing now.

I thanked her and smiled to myself. She'd thought ahead and reserved a ticket for me? Like I was simply a part of their group. I couldn't remember the last time I had a group of friends I didn't have to fight tooth and nail to earn my space in. Where I didn't have to bend over backward to be included.

This was how it was supposed to be, a tiny voice reminded me. The people I thought were my friends through middle school, high school, and college took advantage of me. It took me two years of being in the real world to see that.

That part of me, the wounded girl, expected the same

thing to happen with Jess and her group. After all, if anyone was in a position to make demands of the people around them, it was professional athletes and their posses. That wasn't the case, at least not for the Fury players I'd met so far.

I sent Kerry another message letting her know I'd be at the game and to come up with a plan to allow us to run into each other without being too obvious, then the meeting ended. I walked out with Jonathan, but he was staring at his phone.

"Will you get Ben? I need to have him check something for me." He went into his office before I could reply.

I sat down and dialed Ben's extension.

"Hi, Vivian." He sounded like he was having a good morning. I hoped I wasn't about to be the accomplice in ruining it.

"Hey, Jonathan asked for you to come check on something for him. Do you have time now, or should I let him know you'll be by later?"

He sighed. "I'm on my way."

I hung up and opened my laptop. Another text from Jess came in during my short walk to my desk. I read it. Then again. And again. *Is it okay if I give out your number?*

Who would want my number?

"Hey? Is he ready?"

I glanced up and smiled at Ben. "Yeah, he's inside."

"Thanks." He passed by, and I went back to the mystery on my computer. All she asked was if it was okay if she gave out my number. To who? One of the women in the Pride? One of the players? A client?

To who?

I asked for an explanation then tried to move on to my actual work, but Kerry sent me an email with plans for her and her date to get food, and me running into them at the arena. It was much simpler than I expected from her, but I agreed and told her to pick a time and location, and I would make sure I was there.

My phone rang, the one on my desk, and I answered it using my professional voice. "This is Vivian."

"Um, hi, Viv." I stared down at the number, confused. It was a transferred call from our receptionist, Erin. She only let it ring through directly without telling me who was calling if it was someone she thought I knew.

"Sorry, who is this?" I lifted my shoulder to hold the phone in place while I typed Erin an instant message asking for details.

"Parker."

I racked my brain for a Parker that would be calling. None of the members of the board or any of Jonathan's family members had that name.

"From the Fury?" He replied.

Erin replied *your friend???*

I ignored that while trying to figure out what was going on. "Oh sorry, Parker. I just wasn't expecting your call."

Was this who Jess was talking about? Why didn't she give him my cell number? Did she even have my work number? Obviously not if it went through Erin rather than directly to my desk.

"I know, sorry. I wasn't sure how to get a hold of you."

So, maybe it wasn't him that asked Jess.

"No problem. What's up?" I peeked over my shoulder, but Jonathan and Ben were focused on something on the screen in front of them.

"I was wondering if you were going to be home this evening."

That caught me off-guard, and I let out a small huff. "I should be, yes. I don't think I have any plans."

"Would it be okay if I stopped by?" His voice was so timid. Like he was nervous. Was he asking me on a date? Could it be counted as a date if he invited himself over?

"Yeah, I'm usually home by five-thirty." Unless I stopped for dinner on the way. I did a mental inventory of our fridge. No, there was some chicken and veggies I could heat up.

"Great, I'll see you later."

He ended the call, and I put the phone back before dropping my hands in my lap. What the heck was that?

Erin sent three more messages asking if the guy wasn't who he said he was and if I needed help. I told her it was fine and checked that the men were still busy before standing and hurrying across the floor to Kerry's desk. I carefully glanced into Simon's office, but he wasn't there.

"Hey, what brings you over?" She grinned and stopped typing when she saw me.

I pulled one of the empty chairs near the entrance to another meeting room over and sat close enough that I could whisper without anyone overhearing, not that anyone ever wandered over to this area.

"Parker called me."

Her eyes narrowed. "The new guy?"

I nodded. I'd told her briefly about helping Jess and Dani set up and how I met some more of the players. "Yeah, he and his roommate, Mitch, were at the dinner party on Friday, so I saw him again there too."

"Okay, so why'd he call?"

I held up a hand, "First off, he called here."

Her head shot back. "Like your desk?"

"No, the mainline. Erin transferred him to me, and I had no idea who it was. I thought it was some investor or something I'd forgotten about."

She shifted in her seat. "So what did he want?"

"To see if I was going to be home tonight."

One of her brows rose. "For what?"

"I'm not sure," I admitted. "Maybe he left something the other night? He just asked if he could stop by, and that was it."

"Maybe he likes you?" She smiled.

The insecure teenager version of me instantly squashed that idea. He was too handsome and fit and famous to be interested in a girl like me.

But I shut her up. I was a beautiful, kind, moderately fun person. I'd dated plenty of attractive men that liked me, all of me. And not in a creepy, fetish way. Not all men were so shallow that they judged based on your dress size.

"I don't know. I didn't get that vibe from him. He was nice, but Mitch made a lot more of an effort to talk to me."

She shrugged. "Men are strange. You never know what's going on in those heads."

"True." I agreed. There was no way of knowing his reasons until tonight. "Jess also texted me, asking if it was okay to give out my number, so at first, I thought he was the one she was talking about, but she would have given him my cell not the mainline to my office."

She pursed her lips, "So there are now two callers."

"What?" I breathed out a laugh.

"Like gentlemen suitors. Didn't they call them callers?"

"I think so, but you're the romance reader. Plus, the other one might not be a gentleman. I've got to wait to see what Jess says." I stood and moved the chair back. "I'll keep you updated."

"You better have more details by lunch."

I thanked her and headed back to my desk. This was way too much excitement for a Monday morning.

I had one text from my roommate waiting. *Mitch asked Lance for your number but wanted to check if that was okay before giving it to him.*

Mitch? I didn't expect him to be the type to ask around. I would have thought he'd be more direct than that.

I told her it was okay and tried to focus for the rest of the morning, but my mind was several blocks away at the Fury arena.

8

PARKER

I second-guessed myself with each footstep from my car to Viv's door. When I decided during practice to call her, I didn't think it would be that big of a deal. We'd hung out twice, well kind of. We'd seen each other twice, and both had been nice enough. We clearly got along, so why was it so weird to call her?

Maybe I should have asked Lance or Mikey for her number. I could have even asked Amelia or headed up to the front office to ask Taylor or Chloe, but I thought that was lame. This wasn't high school where I went through a girl's friends to talk to her. I looked up the company she said she worked for and asked for her, telling the woman who answered that I was a friend. Viv didn't seem to remember me without having to tell her I was on the team. Maybe I wasn't as memorable to her as I thought.

Oh well. It was too late. I knocked on the door, and it opened a moment later. Viv let me in with a wide grin. She looked comfortable in an oversized University of Utah sweatshirt and leggings.

"How are you?" she asked while leading us to the kitchen.

Her place looked different from the night of the party. It had been one big open space then, but now the area was separated into a dining room and living room with a cozy, mismatched style that mirrored her bedroom. I liked all the different colored quilts draped over the two turquoise couches and the gold and white dining room table that looked like it was actually vintage rather than a remake.

"Good." I stopped at the end of the kitchen counter and leaned against it.

Her smile stayed in place while she watched me. "Would you like something to drink? Have you eaten? I don't have a ton on hand. I should have gone to the grocery store over the weekend, but I can grill some chicken and veggies."

I waved her off. "No, I'm fine. I'll take a glass of water though."

She turned and filled a bright yellow cup with a pitcher from the fridge and offered it to me.

"Thanks."

There were a few moments of silence, and I realized she was waiting on me. Right, she was wondering why I was here.

"Is everything okay?" she finally asked.

"Yeah, I just wanted to talk."

Her brows rose a fraction of an inch before she recovered. "About?"

I eyed the living room and she crossed over and took a seat on one end and I sat on the opposite, resting against an orange and yellow blanket. Her expression was open, waiting for me to start.

"As you know, I don't know many people here." I paused and stared down at my glass. "I've been fine with that in the past. I didn't have many close friends on my last team, or the team before. I thought that what I needed to do was keep to myself and play the best I could. That was all that mattered."

"But now?" she asked.

"Now, I can see that the Fury is different. There are a few guys that hang on the outskirts and don't really get involved off the ice, but I don't want that. This team is about being a family and relying on each other and being there for one another."

Her eyes crinkled. "That's good. I'd rather be on a team like that."

"Me too," I admitted. "I just don't know how to be that kind of player, or person."

She cocked her head. "You don't know how to be more involved?"

I nodded.

"Well, it looks like you've already started. You showed up with Mitch when Jess and Dani needed help. That shows you're a team player and want to be there for the others. Then you came to the dinner party. That was another step in the right direction."

"Yeah." I sighed. I wished I was better at this, talking. Opening up to someone, but this was new to me.

She leaned forward. "Parker, why are you talking to me about this?"

Why indeed. I was beginning to second guess myself. It didn't make sense, but I told her the truth. "Because when I decided I wanted to commit to this, to immersing myself, you were the first person I thought of."

She quirked her mouth like she didn't quite believe me. "Why? I'm not even a part of the group. I'm only invited to some things because of Jess."

I shook my head. "That's not true. Maybe it started that way, but from a true outsider's perspective, you're just as much a member of the Pride as any of the other women."

"Even if that were true, which I don't think it is, there are still better people to talk to. Chloe or Emma seem to really be clued in. Jake and Jason have been on the team for a while. Even Lance, but I guess he's new to the more settled-down side of the team."

Those were more logical options, but I thought of her first. That meant something. My subconscious trusted her or something.

"I will talk to them, but I wanted to meet with you first. You've become part of the group recently, so you know how."

She laughed. "It's not like there's some special ritual you have to go through. Just be yourself."

I stared over at the coffee table covered with coasters with vintage ads on them and scooted one closer to use for my water.

"You're right. I guess I just wanted a friend here."

She straightened, and I was struck with the feeling I'd said something horribly wrong. "Why?"

"Why do I want to be your friend?"

"Yes." She held my stare.

"Why does anyone want to be friends with someone else? They like them and want to be around them. Everyone seems to really like you. You make people comfortable."

She narrowed her eyes. "I've been *the friend* before. Most of my life, actually."

How was I messing this up? It was like we were saying and hearing the same words but finding completely different meanings.

"I'm the one that men like enough to hang out with until someone better or prettier or more exciting comes along."

My mouth dropped a bit. She thought I was going to use her and toss her away? Had that happened before?

I froze. That was what I was doing. I needed something from her, but I didn't want her to think I was just going to leave her behind the second I didn't she wasn't useful. I couldn't imagine what kind of person would do that to her.

"I promise, Vivi. That's not what I'm trying to do--"

She interrupted me. "There's always something that my so-called *friend* is after. So what is it?"

I shook my head. This wasn't going how I had planned. I thought we'd laugh and joke as easily as she did with Mitch, or she might even be as eager to be friends as I was. "It's just that I'm new here, and you're kind of new to the group too. I thought we could be friends and navigate it together."

She didn't immediately say no which was a minor victory. "I'm not some tool to get into the group. You're already in on your own. You're on the team."

She was going to make me spell it out for her. I sat up straight and met her eyes. "I like you, Viv. You're kind and thoughtful and very supportive of your friends. You're funny and know how to put people at ease. Things are different here. The guys are different. I used to be fine on my own. I didn't think I was missing out as long as I did my best and showed up for the team, but being around these guys and the Pride, I realized there's more. I'm missing out on connections and experiences, and I don't want to keep doing that."

She let out a humorless laugh. "Exactly, so why me? You should be spending time with the guys. I'm not actually connected to the team."

I sank into the couch. "Honestly. I'm not sure how to make that happen."

"What do you mean?" she asked.

"I don't know how to make friends," I admitted.

"You're doing it now." She waved her hand between us.

I dipped my chin to meet her eyes. "You're different."

Her gaze seemed to pierce into me. "How?"

"There isn't pressure. I don't have to worry about messing up and ostracizing myself from the team."

She leaned back. "You don't think there would be consequences for messing up with me?"

This woman was not giving me an inch of slack. "That's not what I meant. I don't know how to do this. I haven't had a friend outside of hockey since I was fourteen."

"So you're practicing on me?"

"Maybe?" I winced.

She stared at the ceiling. "I don't want to play that role for you."

"What are you talking about?" It was like we were having two different conversations with very minimal overlap.

"I'm not here for your entertainment. I'm not the funny fat girl, sitting around, waiting for a crumb of attention before I jump up and roll over to beg for more."

I was stunned. There were no words. Was this really what she thought of me? Of herself?

"Don't deny it, Parker. I've been in this spot countless times before. I used to do it, too, but I'm not an insecure little girl anymore. I'm not going to allow myself to be used for your personal gain. Your *friendship* will end the second you get what you want, and I'll end up forgotten or hurt."

"I––No. Viv, that's not at all what I meant." I was struggling to find words to make her understand.

"Oh, really? Then how did you think this would play out?" Her eyes were pleading with mine to change her mind. To prove her wrong.

I swallowed and tried to articulate what I'd been thinking about. "We could hang out when we're both available. Get dinners or see a movie. If there's a team event, you could come with me. If you have any parties or anything, you could bring me along. I know you don't know me that well, but I'm asking from a genuine place. I don't have a malicious agenda."

"I want to believe you but––"

I cut her off. "Give me a shot. A trial run."

"What?"

"Try this out with me for a week or two."

"What are you talking about?"

I leaned forward. She wasn't saying no, so there was a chance to get her to hear me without wanting to slap me. "We'll exchange numbers, and for the next fourteen days, we'll act as each other's friend."

She raised a brow. "I have plenty of friends."

"I know." I swallowed. "But I don't."

She sat back, and her challenging look disappeared, making my heart race. Did she finally get it? Had I said the right thing to make her understand?

"You're really terrible at this." Her voice had softened.

"I know."

She almost smiled. I saw the corner of her mouth twitch but stop. "Want to know how normal people become friends?"

I nodded.

"They get your number and send a text like—" She reached for her phone, pulled up her text messages, and read, "Would you like to get dinner this week? Wednesday and Friday work best for me."

"Wasn't that basically what I did?"

She actually laughed. "No. You called my work and set up whatever this is." She gestured between us. "And made it a super awkward situation."

"Oh." Her rejection was coming.

She sighed and cocked her head while studying me. "Two weeks."

I straightened. "Really?"

"Yes, but be prepared for any notes or critique I may have."

"Yes. Absolutely."

She watched me for a moment with an almost sad expression. "And don't make me regret this."

"I'll try not to." I wanted to promise her, but we both knew those would be empty words. She cared about actions, not words. This was my chance to prove myself. I was going to show her she could depend on me. That I was there for her just as much as I needed her. After two weeks, this whole thing would be something we could laugh about. The ridiculous beginning of our long friendship.

It wasn't until later that night I wondered who the text she read was from. Someone asked her to dinner. That sounded a lot like a date. I glanced at my phone. A friend could ask who it was with. I could even ask so I knew what night she was free to hang out. I picked up my phone and sent the message before I could change my mind.

Did you decide on Wednesday or Friday?

It didn't matter who she was going out with, even if the thought made me more uncomfortable than it should. Friends supported each other.

9

VIVIAN

I should have asked if Parker had ever been in a relationship of any sort, romantic or platonic. He was rusty in the communication department, and it was only the morning of day one. He asked me what day I was free because my other friend asked me to go to dinner. I told him we were going on Wednesday, and he never replied.

Did he get the information he wanted so he was done? Why didn't he ask any follow-up questions? Or tell me to have fun. Something to make it feel like an actual conversation based on genuine curiosity and wanting to be a part of the other person's life rather than a single-minded quest for information.

He wasn't lying when he said he didn't have many friends. I added him on my two preferred social media accounts, but he didn't accept. I could see enough of his profile to figure out he didn't use them. Fans that created accounts about him, or on his behalf, gave me better insight into who he was than the man himself. This also told me he was popular enough to have dedicated fans that followed him through the trade. All of the information about him online had been updated to his move to Salt Lake and the Fury team. I doubted he'd even had his picture taken in his new jersey yet, but someone had photoshopped a decent version to add to one of the more popular profiles.

According to another social media page, Parker had never had a girlfriend, at least publicly, and most people chalked it up to his dedication to his sport and the time restraints. That would have been a fair enough assessment before I met so many of the Fury players. They had families and relationships just like anyone else. Sure, they had to travel during the season, but so did many professions. They also got summers off, with only personal training to demand their time and attention.

It was perfectly possible for him to have a girlfriend, so why weren't there any exes?

Just another question to add to my ever-growing list. The next time we saw each other, I was digging in. I planned to show him just what it was like to be friends with a girl. I'd pry and pester until I knew him as well as I knew Kerry or Jess. Then we'd really see how serious he was about continuing this trial.

First, I needed to do what real friends do. Confide in Jess about how weird this whole thing was. I mentioned it to Kerry, but she was too starstruck and a little too in love with Parker's face to focus on my dilemma. She thought I was rash and not giving him enough of a chance. She was wrong. Giving him a chance was exactly what I was doing.

We were meeting for lunch so I could catch her up. She had an event tonight so she wouldn't be home early enough for us to talk. Since things were busy, she couldn't get away to talk alone, but I didn't mind having another opinion, so I brought lunch for her and Dani.

"You're a lifesaver!" Dani clapped when I walked into their office with three bags of burgers and fries. "Grease and carbs are the only things that will keep me going until midnight. I love you."

"Thanks for letting me interrupt. I know you guys are busy." I unpacked my bag as Jess came into their conference room and fell into the nearest chair.

"We needed a break." She sighed and leaned forward as dramatically as possible. "I'm famished."

Dani took a big bite and moaned with her eyes closed. "Delicious," she mumbled with a full mouth.

I unwrapped my burger and almost drooled. It was rare that I ate something so glutenous but after my first bite of gooey, cheesy meat, I felt nothing but bliss. "Oh, this was a good idea."

Jess nodded. "I had a feeling we needed the big guns today." She started eating, then raised her brows. "So tell us what's going on."

"Oh, yes!" Dani perked up. "Jess said something happened."

"Well, Parker called me at work yesterday and asked to come over." I told them about the conversation we had and my reservations. They listened intently, eating while I confessed I wasn't sure how to feel about the arrangement. "The only thing that made me agree was that it's only two weeks. After that, I can point out the many ways it's not working and we can both move on. Maybe by then, he'll feel more comfortable on the team and not feel like he needs someone to hold his hand."

"You think that's what he's doing?" Jess asked.

I agreed. "Yeah. Why else would he come over and explicitly ask to be friends?"

"He's a strange duck," Dani said with a small smile. "He really doesn't get how strange that is?"

"I guess not. I read him the text Mitch sent me asking to go out to dinner, and I said that's what normal people do and he blew by it. Well, that's not true. Last night he texted me asking what day I was going so he would know what day I was free."

Jess cocked her head. "But he didn't ask who sent you the message?"

"Nope." It was all so weird.

"So he doesn't know Mitch, his roommate, asked for your number and asked to go to dinner with you?" Dani summarized.

"Yeah," I replied.

They both shook their heads.

"Men. I don't understand them," Jess said.

"Maybe it means that friendship is really what he's interested in. If he was jealous, he would have asked for more information."

"He's not jealous." I stopped that thought before the women could spiral out of control. "It was pretty clear he doesn't see me as a potential romantic prospect. I doubt he's even noticed I'm a woman, at this point."

Jess rolled her eyes. "It's pretty hard not to see that."

I huffed. "What's that supposed to mean?"

She waved her hand up and down where I was sitting. "You've got the va-va-voom going on. You're like one of those fifties pin-up girls with all those curves."

I tried to take the words as the compliment she intended, but pointing out my curves had been most people's default my whole life. Like if they focused on my butt and boobs, they could ignore the other, less flattering, areas of my body that were just as curvaceous, like my stomach, hips, and thighs. I was plus-sized. My whole life I'd been bigger than the other girls my age, and up until recently, it was the major source of my insecurity and self-loathing. It had only been in the past year or so, as I focused on being healthy rather than skinny, that I learned to love my body.

"I'm thankful for your interpretation but––"

"Don't even start in on you thinking he wouldn't be interested in you for more than friendship," Dani said in her stern, boss-lady voice.

I put my hand up to stop her. "Honestly, I appreciate what you're saying, but it's not the vibe I get from him. I'm not being self-conscious. I genuinely don't think he's attracted to me that way, and it's perfectly fine. We all have our preferences. I'm not offended."

Jess cocked a brow. "So you think he came to you to ask to be friends without anything else in mind?"

"At first I thought there was some other ulterior motive. In the past when men have gotten close to me, it's been to use me to get something else. In school, it was for me to introduce them to my friends. In college, it was the same, plus I had a few beautiful roommates that guys tried to use me for an introduction. They'd flirt with me or buy me drinks in hopes I'd set them up, like I was some sort of wingman. With Parker, I can't think of what he would want. He doesn't know about my best friend, Kerry, and you guys are all taken, so I don't know what it would be."

Dani popped a fry into her mouth and chewed with a thoughtful expression. "Okay, so he meets you on like his second day here. Sees you interacting with the guys from the team. Even become friends with Mitch that night, and thinks hey, that's someone I want to know?" She ate another fry. "I can see it."

"And he's just awkward enough to go about it in the strangest, most uncomfortable way possible," Jess added.

"Right," I agreed.

"So, what's the problem? If we move past how weird he is," Dani asked.

I sighed. "There were these alarms going off in my head. Maybe it's just the past haunting me, but something told me that I need to protect myself. That I'm the one that's going to end up hurt. That this whole game is going to cost me."

Jess's expression turned serious. "Why do you think you'll get hurt? If he's just asking to be your friend, you only have something to gain."

How could I explain this to them without sounding insecure? "It feels like taking a step back. Like ignoring all the work I've done on myself to allow someone to have power enough to influence me and my feelings."

"You're scared of being vulnerable?" Dani watched me.

That was a more concise way of explaining it. "Yeah, I guess so."

"You didn't feel like that when you met me?" Jess asked.

I shook my head. "No."

"Or when you met me and the guys and the rest of the team?" Dani followed up.

I picked up a napkin and rubbed my hands. "I was nervous, sure, but not in the way I am now. It didn't feel like you had the potential to break me. Like, worst-case scenario, we didn't click and I didn't come around to your office or the games anymore."

They shared a look.

"You think Parker has the potential to break you?" Jess asked.

Crap. That sort of slipped out, but it was true. "Yeah."

"Why?" Her voice was gentle, not challenging.

"As I said, it feels like I'm falling back into old habits even though I know better and it's not the same thing. I just don't want to be that girl again. I want to be the main character of my own story, and for the past twenty-three years, I've been the sidekick."

Dani lifted a hand to her mouth, and Jess simply stared. I didn't know what else to say. Those were words I'd only ever thought before, never ever daring to admit aloud, and now I just poured them at the feet of two friends that hadn't seen this side of me before. I was grateful for to have someone to tell. They didn't know my history. They only got to see the new, happy version of me. Showing them this sliver of who I once was scared me.

"Oh, Viv." Dani gave me a sad look. "Everyone deserves to be the main character, and you are. The person you're talking about isn't the woman I know. You're strong and determined and confident. You're magnetic. There's a reason we've all clicked with you and why you've been brought into the fold, despite not dating one of the guys. We all love being around you. You give and you're thoughtful, but you also let others be the givers. You're balanced."

Jess nodded. "Magnetic is the perfect word. You draw people in and make them feel important, and you form real connections. That's so rare, and it's one of the reasons I wanted to move in with you. The second we met, I knew I wanted to be around you."

I smiled, grateful for their compliments. It didn't feel like they were talking just to be nice. They truly felt this way.

"That's probably how Parker feels, he just doesn't know how to articulate it," Dani said.

I replayed the conversation with him in my head. "He did say some things like that."

"Exactly." She gave me a knowing look. "I think you need to give yourself and him a bit more credit. He doesn't want to be friends for some sort of trick or bait and switch. He saw someone that's like sunlight. He can't help but want to be around your warmth," Jess said.

I leaned forward with my elbows on the counter. "Thanks, guys. I didn't realize how much I needed to hear that."

"We all get lost in our own heads from time to time. Don't sell yourself short." Dani smiled.

"Plus, we have your date with Mitch to discuss." Jess winked.

I held up my hand. "It's not a date. It's just dinner."

Dani bit her lips, and Jess winked before shrugging. I had a feeling they were up to something, but I decided I didn't want to know. I was back to feeling good again, so I sent Parker a text asking how his day was going, as a friend would, and cleaned up.

10

PARKER

Pulling on my maroon and black jersey still felt off. Not wrong, just weird. I was so used to seeing myself in white and gold that any time I caught myself in a mirror, I paused. It was only my second game with the Fury, and I predicted that by the fifth or sixth I wouldn't even think about it.

That was the nature of our jobs. Adapt. Change. Be prepared for the floor to be swept out from under you and get back up in seconds.

The biggest unknown was how to act off the ice.

The men around me were hyping each other up, chanting and slapping one another on the shoulders while I sat in front of my locker with headphones in. They had their routine, and I had mine. One day, hopefully soon, they would be the same.

It wasn't like I was the only one that chose to be quiet before a game. Three, no four, others had their eyes closed or headphones on, blocking out the chaos around them. None of the loud group seemed to mind us not participating. I wished they did. I wished they forced me to stand up and get in the middle of it all. It was pathetic that I needed that push, but I'd always been this way. Tell me where to go and when, and I'd do it without a single question. But tell me to go and do what I want, and I'll flounder. I need direction. I need someone else to take charge. There was a reason I never made captain of any team I'd ever been on. I wasn't a natural-born leader. Center stage held no appeal. Having any more attention on me than was completely necessary made my skin crawl.

All I ever wanted was to do my part as well as I could. As long as I was where I needed to be there for my teammates, I was happy. I didn't care about scoring records. I didn't care about my personal stats at all. My ego was quelled before it had the chance to develop. I was taught from my very first team that there was no room on the ice for individuals. Only a team. I'd remembered that every single day since. I wasn't here for my own glory. I wanted my team to win.

A hand waved in front of my face, and I blinked before looking up to see Wyatt Hartman smiling down at me. "What's got you so locked up in that head of yours, Garrison?"

I could feel eyes on me and realized then that more than half of the guys were watching us. I didn't particularly want to admit I was rehashing pep talks from my mini mite days. The only other thought I'd had all day was of Vivian and her good luck text from this morning. She seemed to have taken over the reins of our friendship, and I wasn't complaining. She texted me the past three days, and if I didn't respond how she thought I should, she told me I killed the conversation and that I had to try again. I was learning to ask more questions as well as giving her more detailed responses.

"Um, nothing." I dropped my gaze to the floor, hoping he would move on. Now that he was actually trying to pull me into the pre-game hype, I just wanted to be left alone.

"Oh, I know that voice." Erik Schultz appeared next to the captain.

"Sounds like girl problems," Reese Murray confirmed from the other side of Hartman.

"Already? You've been here, what, a week?" Hartman said with a laugh.

I nodded.

"And already got lady troubles," Schultz said with a knowing look. "I don't know if I'm impressed or concerned."

"Impressed," Murray said.

"Yeah, who else got mixed up that fast?" Schultz chuckled.

At first, I thought they were mad, or laughing at me, but when Hartman clapped me on the back, I realized they were commiserating with me. "We've all been there, man."

Our definitions of lady troubles were likely completely different, but I didn't know how to stop them now that they were going.

"You sure have." Murray bumped Schultz with his elbow. "Dating Coach's daughter was a bold move."

"Eh, it worked out fine," he replied with a cocky grin.

"So, who's the fine woman? Anyone we know?" Hartman asked.

My mind was still spinning from being included in their strange club, and I didn't think before I said her name. "Viv."

"Viv like Vivi? Like Vivian?" Murray repeated.

"Vivian Ashwood," I clarified. "Jess's roommate."

Murray straightened. "You be good to that one. Chloe really likes her, so if you mess with her, you face not only her wrath but the entire Pride's."

Schultz and Hartman confirmed.

"Plus, we like her," Olli Letang called from a few feet away. "So you'll deal with us too."

I wished I could record this to prove to Viv how much everyone here liked her. Then she would finally believe me.

"It's not like that." It was time to explain.

"You and Viv?" Jason appeared and pursed his lips. "I can't say I'm all that surprised. It was only a matter of time before one of the single lads swept her up."

"She's a doll, that one," Letang said with a smile.

"Why are you guys talking like that?" Schultz asked.

They shrugged, and Mitch wandered over. "Did you say something about Viv?"

"Oh yeah, Parker's having problems with her," Murray said before I could open my mouth. "She probably just wants you to come out of your shell more."

I wasn't sure what to say. I never actually said there was a problem, but now I felt self-conscious. What if that was a real issue for her? I was pretty introverted, while she was the type to never meet a stranger.

"I didn't know you two––" Mitch began. His tone sounded off.

"It's time, Fury!" Coach Rust walked in, ending our conversation.

I wanted to ask Mitch why he was so interested, but it would have to wait until after the game.

We marched down the hall and, one by one, stepped onto the ice as cheers erupted from the crowd. The energy soaked into every inch of me, getting me ready to play like no speech, song, or ritual could. This was what I lived for. This was why I trained so hard and pushed my body to the limits day after day. The fans' reactions to just seeing us was fuel to the fire in my soul. I wouldn't give this up until I literally couldn't keep going. It was the least they deserved for loving and supporting us even on our darkest days.

"Heads up." Hartman bumped into me, then pointed to a section of the audience. It was where the Pride sat. Mitch pointed it out to me on the last game, but I didn't think much of it. I had no reason to then, but now I searched the rows until I found Viv's face. She was waving and grinning like the women around her. I waved, and she jumped up and down a bit.

If I wasn't careful, I'd let her presence distract me tonight, and that wasn't why I was here. She was just one in the thousands. I couldn't think about her, our complicated friendship, or the guys' assumption that there was something going on between us. That could all be dealt with later.

The whistle blew, and I went back to the bench for the opening ceremony. Jason tapped on my shoulder to tell me to scoot down as the game started, and we sat down.

"Get a point tonight," he said just loud enough for me to hear.

"That's the goal every game," I countered.

"I'll give you a hundred if you can pull off an assist tonight." He wagged his brows.

As a left wing, that was my primary function. Get the puck from the center, shoot, score. It wasn't like I was out there for kicks and giggles, but if he wanted to give me a hundred bucks, I wasn't going to turn him down.

"Sure." I agreed, and he knocked my helmet.

After four minutes of play, we stood for our line change.

"Oh and I meant get an assist before me," he called as he hopped on the ice and skated into position.

I almost laughed. Since he was the right wing on my line, we'd have pretty equal footing. He wanted to turn up the competition? That was fine. I slapped my stick down, and Brandon Cullen, our center, gave me a nod. He knew I was ready and hungry for this.

When we got back on the bench after three minutes of play, after bumping gloves with the team, Jason laughed and hit the back of my helmet. "Double or nothing?"

I shrugged. "Sure."

It was tough to keep my composure and not break out in a giddy grin. Brandon and I had pulled off a perfect play that ended in him scoring, with me getting a point for the assist. Jason might as well have not even been out there.

"Keep it up, Garrison." Hartman commended from down the bench.

I nodded, reveling in the praise from my captain and teammates.

I hadn't done anything I wouldn't have normally, but I guess showing my intention and taking the initiative with Brandon was what pushed us and helped us score so quickly. I couldn't wait to test my theory on our next rotation.

By the end of the game, I had not one point but two. I wasn't sure I won the bet, though, since my second assist was with Jason, who scored.

Either way, the team won, and that was what mattered.

"Nice work out there," Coach Romney said as I passed him on my way into the locker room.

"Way to go, Garrison," a voice called.

"Not bad," another said.

"Two points on your second game. I'm impressed," Schultz said on his way to his locker.

Suddenly, I wasn't just the new guy. Not only were they calling me by my name, but commending me. Most of these guys were three-time champions. I thought it would take months to earn their respect.

I turned to Jason and eyed him. "Thanks, man."

"Don't thank me. I'm not giving you a dollar. That was a tie." He ran his towel over his sweaty face.

"I know, but still. Thanks."

He paused before finally nodding. He knew what he did, even if it was under the guise of a bet. He found a natural way to push me to show off and prove myself to the team. I appreciated that more than he would ever know.

"Hurry and clean up, boys! We're going to the Pie tonight!" Hartman called.

Cheers broke out, and I looked around for someone to explain.

Murray must have seen my confusion. "It's the best pizza place in town. On game nights, especially the ones we win, they know to keep their back room reserved for us. You in?"

I was being invited. To their celebration. "Of course."

"Cool, let me know if you need a ride." He left for the showers, and I caught Mitch.

"Hey, are you going?" I asked.

He shrugged. "I don't normally."

"Oh." I wasn't sure what else to say. He was my ride. Would it be rude to tell him I was going with someone else? Maybe I could go home and get my own car.

"But you did have a great night. What kind of roommate would I be if I didn't go celebrate with you?"

I grinned. "Thanks, man."

By the time we were showered, dressed, and through the press waiting for interviews, the women of the Pride had made their way down to the tunnels. I tried to be discreet while looking for Viv, but it didn't take long to see her running up to Mitch. She threw her arms around him, and he caught her.

"That was amazing! You were so great out there." She looked up at him with adoration I couldn't explain. Just how close were they? I thought they only met two times.

"Thanks, it was a pretty good night." He paused and turned around with his arm over her shoulders. "Right, Garrison. You had a pretty impressive night."

"Thanks." I tried to smile, but my focus was on where he was touching her.

"You were really great." Vivi focused on me. "I can't believe how fast you are. It was almost as hard to keep track of you as it is the puck."

Before I could respond, Mitch took her attention. "Do you want to come to the Pie with us? Everyone's going to celebrate."

"I'd love to. Jess and Emma told me all about it." She beamed at each of us. I noticed then she was wearing a Fury hoodie, not a jersey like all the other women. Did she not have one? Maybe she didn't know who's to wear. The perfect idea came to mind. After all, friends supported each other.

11

VIVIAN

As much fun as it was to watch the guys win and to celebrate with them afterward, I was seriously questioning if it was worth it when I was on my third cup of coffee before ten the next morning. If I wanted to continue going to games with Jess, I was going to have to learn to function on less than eight hours of sleep.

Maybe I would only attend the weekend games, or not go to the dinners with everyone else. But almost all the other women had regular day jobs to get up for. Was there a secret to trudging through the next day? Next time I saw the Pride, I'd ask.

"You okay?" Kerry asked me as she refilled her mug. "You never come back for thirds."

"Just a late night."

"Oh, right," she grinned. "Just a casual hang out with the Fury guys. No big deal."

I rolled my eyes. "It's starting to feel that way. Once the shock and glamour wear off, they're just normal guys."

"Sure," she laughed. "Wyatt Hartman and Erik Schultz

aren't hockey gods, just average Joes you'd run into on the street."

"You should see Erik around his wife and sister. They put him in his place whenever his ego makes an appearance."

"What a life." She sighed wistfully.

One of the guys from the development team was eying us, and I didn't want him to hear more than he already had, so I grabbed her arm and dragged her away. "I don't want the office knowing how I spent my off time."

She nodded. "Fine. I get it. Once word gets out, they'll suddenly act like your best friend for tickets and autographs."

"Exactly," I said.

"It's too bad your real best friend doesn't even get any of those perks."

"You were at the game!" I laughed.

She shrugged. "In the normal people section."

"AJ was really nice." I changed the subject to something I knew she would want to discuss. "I'm glad our plan worked."

She lit up with a brilliant smile. "I'm so glad you got to meet him. I really like him, Vivi."

I could tell that as soon as I saw them walking toward me last night. They were somehow staring into each other's eyes while navigating the crowded lines at concessions, smiling and blushing. They were definitely falling for each other, but I wasn't sure if they knew that yet.

"I'm so happy for you. He seems like a great guy."

She lifted her mug to cover her mouth as if that would hide the effect of what just mentioning him did to her.

"If I ever find someone, we should double. I want to get to know him better." Although with my track record, I doubted I'd meet anyone worthy of meeting my best friend. Luck and dating were two things that hadn't ever come together for me.

"Yes, oh, yes. We definitely should."

This could be the perfect test for Parker. After all, he said we could bring each other to activities if needed.

"Maybe this weekend?" I offered.

She considered. "Sure, but who are you going to bring?"

"Parker?" Was that a terrible idea?

Her eyes glinted with something mischievous. "Good idea. After all, friends go out to dinner all the time."

I resisted the urge to roll my eyes. She was enjoying this trial period more than I was. It probably had to do with seeing me out of my comfort zone, something she was constantly pushing me to do.

"Let me know when you and AJ are free, and I'll check with him."

She did a little happy dance on her way to her desk while I crossed the floor to mine. This wasn't a double date. I'd have to figure out a way to make that clear to everyone involved. It was just an excuse for me to get to know my best friend's love interest better. Parker was coming to balance the numbers.

That night when I got home, there was a white, rectangular box waiting in front of the door. A small note was attached with my name and address written across the back. I carried it inside with me, calling out to see if Jess was home, but she didn't respond.

I took off my coat and hung it up next to my purse before setting the box on the kitchen counter and removing the lid. A Fury jersey was meticulously folded inside in a way that made sure the logo on the front and numbers on the sleeves weren't bent. I lifted it and turned it around. Garrison was stitched across the back. Parker's jersey? I didn't order this.

I carefully laid it flat and took a picture, then sent it to him, asking if he was behind the delivery. I bit my lip, wondering what it meant. My heart raced until my phone lit up with his reply of a simple yes.

One word, and my stomach flipped. He'd thought about me enough to not only want me to wear his number, but he sent it to me?

I touched the slick fabric and smiled. I now had my very own jersey to wear to the games. He must not have thought my hoodie was sufficient. Plus, this took away the decision that had been looming over me of who's jersey to get. I'd been going between Hartman, since he was captain and a safe choice, and Mitch or Parker.

Now I didn't have to make up my mind.

If it wasn't a gift from someone on the team, I would have thought it was too much. Jerseys were expensive. It was why I was waiting to purchase my own until I narrowed it down. The players probably got an allotment or something though. Maybe he just asked Chloe, and she made it happen. That wouldn't have surprised me.

How it happened didn't matter. He thought of me and wanted me to wear his number. That's what friends did.

Well, it was also what wives and girlfriends did. And millions of fans, so maybe it wasn't as personal as I was making it out to be.

I sent him a thank you before taking the jersey to my room and hanging it up. It stood out next to my business casual attire, but I liked the contrast. It was the perfect visual representation of the changes in my life. My world was expanding, and now I had physical proof.

My phone chimed, and I checked it to see a message from Mitch asking if I was home and free. I replied yes to both and a few seconds later, there was a knock at the door.

I hurried to answer it and found him leaning against the door frame, looking uncharacteristically grim. "Hey, come in."

"Thanks," he mumbled and went directly to the couch.

I followed and sat at an angle to face him. "What's going on?"

"I just had to get away." He swallowed. "This was the first place I thought of."

I was touched, but still too concerned to focus on that. "What or who did you need to get away from?"

He rubbed his face. "Myself."

Huh. This was not what I expected from a visit with him. Mitch was one of the most positive people I'd ever met. When we went to dinner, I had a side cramp before the appetizers even arrived from laughing so hard.

"Tell me what's going on." I wanted to reach out to him, but I wasn't sure of what he wanted or needed yet.

"Are we alone?" He glanced up at me.

"Yeah, Jess isn't here. She's been working late this week."

He nodded. "I don't know how much longer I can do this. I know we've only just met, but I can tell you don't care about who I am, as far as being a professional athlete. You've made an effort to actually get to know me. You don't even call me Dory like everyone else."

I shrugged, trying to downplay my anxiety. What did 'do this' mean? "It didn't seem like you liked that name."

"It's fine. Most of the guys have nicknames or go by their last name, but it's nice for someone to actually look at me and see, well, me. Mitch."

I admitted to him at dinner that I'd been intimidated when we first met. Not because of who he was on the ice. I didn't know enough to let that influence me, but he was just so large. He seemed like a force the first time I saw him walk into the ballroom. The man sitting before me was so different from that memory, I was speechless. I hated seeing him in so much pain, but I wasn't sure what to do to help.

"I suppose it's my fault. I've let people see who they wanted to for so long that I fell into that role. I let it become who I was, even though it wasn't true. It was easy to let them think they were right in their assumptions than to step up and correct them."

"I know that feeling all too well." I sighed. Maybe that was why we clicked so easily. We saw a piece of ourselves in each other.

His sorrowful eyes locked on mine. "I'm not sure I can keep up the act anymore."

I didn't know what act he meant, but I leaned forward and took his large, calloused hand in mine. When his body sagged at the contact, I knew I was on the right path. "Then stop. At least around the people closest to you. Let yourself be who you really are. Your friends and family will love you no matter what."

I waited, wanting to go at his pace. He came here to talk. All I had to do was be patient and listen.

"I'm trying." He tightened his fingers around my hand. "I feel like I can be myself with you."

"Me too." I never felt like there was anything but a genuine connection between us.

"I don't even feel like that at home. I have to keep pretending and playing the role that's been constructed for me."

"At home? You mean with Parker?"

He ducked his head. "And any of the guys that lived with me before him. I wanted to live alone for a few months, but Chloe called and said Parker was in a jam, so I agreed to let him move in." His shoulders slumped and met my eyes, "Don't get me wrong. I like him. It's just I wish I had space to myself."

I could understand that. There were a few weeks before Jess moved in that I was alone and it was really nice until I got lonely again.

"What role do you feel like you're playing?" I pressed, hoping it wasn't too soon to ask.

He rolled his lips together so tightly they turned white. "I've only told a few people this." He sucked in a breath and slowly let it out. "I'm gay."

I waited for him to continue, but he watched me without breathing. "Okay."

His eyes widened. "That's it?"

I nodded. "Yes?"

He let out an enormous sigh. "You're not going to freak out?"

"Nope." I smiled just a bit at his confusion. My heart ached that he was so afraid of sharing this part of himself with me. I didn't want to think about what made him so hesitant. "Mitch, that's one part of you. It doesn't change who you are or how I see you."

He turned his head away from me, and the tension and weight that he'd walked in with slowly lifted from his shoulders.

"Do the guys on the team know?" I asked.

"No." He stared out the balcony windows. "My family does and most of my friends at the boxing gym."

It was a relief that he had some support.

"I was told by a coach when I was young, maybe twelve or thirteen, that I couldn't come out to my teammates. That it would make them uncomfortable or alienate me from them." He cleared his throat. "I know that isn't right or how things should be, but it stuck with me. The last thing I ever want to do is make any of them see me differently."

I scooted closer and squeezed his hand. After a second, he finally faced me. "If any of them do, that's on them, not you. Plus, you've been sacrificing your own comfort for how many years? I think you should give them some credit. I have a feeling they'll react better than whatever you have created in your head."

He didn't say anything for a moment. "You're probably right."

I waited until he met my eyes. "I'm not saying you have to tell them. That's one hundred percent up to you if or when you tell them, but I really think they would like to have the option to support you."

He leaned back against the pillows. "I didn't mean to keep it from them for this long. It's just none of them ever asked, and I didn't feel like I had to tell them. Now it's been two years, and the longer I wait, the bigger it feels."

"I've felt that before. Something small just grows and festers until it's this monumental thing in your mind."

"Exactly. I wouldn't even know how to try to start now. I don't want them to think I was hiding it from them, but I guess I was." He paused. "It's something to worry about at another time. I'm glad I told you though."

"Me too, Mitch." I wrapped my arms around his middle, holding him as tight as I could.

"You're still my highlander."

He shook with a short laugh. "What?"

I bit my lip. "That's what I thought the first time I saw you. You look like a Scottish man that should be out throwing logs and lifting boulders."

He snorted and twisted to look at me. "Thank you, Vivi. You just made my day."

12

PARKER

Since I knew Vivian was home, I decided to head over to her place after I finished cleaning up following an extra training session with Brandon and Jason. We worked on a few passing drills after the team's normal practice and then headed into the weight room for another hour. It had been brutal, but if they were willing to go the extra mile, then I was determined to meet them step for step. Well, not literally. The last thing I wanted to do was run, but neither did they.

I knocked on her door and waited, only second-guessing my impromptu drop-by for a second. If she was busy, that was fine. I'd just head home. Stopping by unannounced was what friends did, hopefully. I was still learning the rules.

Finally, it swung open, and she looked surprised for a moment before catching herself. "Parker, hi."

She was talking louder than necessary, and I realized I might be interrupting something. She glanced toward the living room, and I followed the movement before freezing.

Mitch?

What was he doing here?

I looked between them. Was I walking in on something? Were they . . .? Her and Mitch? I never would have guessed . . . I couldn't even think clearly.

"Hey, Parker," Mitch called out, which seemed to break whatever spell Vivi had been under.

"Sorry, come in. We were just chatting." She seemed nervous. Were they doing more than talking? I mean, I shouldn't have been that surprised, if so. They had a connection the first night they met. I witnessed it happen. I just didn't realize they were more than friends.

I'd been an idiot. She was beautiful. Stunning, actually, with a personality to match. She could be sweet or sassy. Not knowing when the switch would flip was half the appeal of being around her. How could I have thought I was the only one to realize that? I was a fool. I'd been texting her, trying to hang out with her, I even sent her my jersey, and she'd been dating Mitch this whole time.

We were friends, only. She was free to date whomever she wanted.

"Sorry, I didn't mean to just barge in. I should have called." I ran my palms over my jeans. The confidence I felt on the way over vanished.

"It's cool, man. I need to head out anyway." Mitch stood and gave Vivi a hug before passing me with a slap on my shoulder. "I'll see you later."

When the door shut behind him, I felt like I was finally able to take a full breath. "I didn't mean for him to leave."

She waved me off. "We really were done, and he mentioned having dinner plans."

It was strange for her to know more about my roommate than I did. "Oh."

She studied me. "Why are you acting so weird?"

"I'm not," I lied.

"You are." She narrowed her eyes. "Did you think you were my *only* friend?"

I ignored her and sat down on the far side of the couch.

"You know, you're allowed to have more than one friend, Parker." Viv put her hands on her hips. "I have enough room in my heart for you and Mitch. Plus, Jess and Kerry and the other girls from the Pride."

"Ha ha." How did she know I was feeling insecure about this?

She grinned and dropped onto the couch. "Thanks again for the jersey. I can't wait to wear it."

I appreciated her topic change. "I'm excited to know that there's at least one person wearing it in the crowd." But if she and Mitch were an item, would she even wear it?

She laughed. "If there aren't more people this week, then it's just a matter of time if you keep playing like you did."

Her compliment meant more to me than when it came from the coaches or my captain. Why? Why did her words and opinion hit me so differently?

"I have a favor to ask you." She looked down at her hands. Was she nervous? I couldn't fathom it. "Kerry, my other best friend"—she shot me a look, and I rolled my eyes— "is dating a new guy, and she really likes him. I said I would go to dinner with them, and it turned into a double date thing. I was wondering if you'd come with me, but it wouldn't be a date for us, obviously."

Yeah, obviously. That stung. Was it because she didn't see me that way or because of Mitch? I shook it off and agreed. "I'd love to."

"Great, we're planning on Friday night since you have a game on Saturday."

"Sounds good." I was only slightly panicking. I'd barely figured out how to be around her and act normally. Now she wanted to add in two strangers?

I'd survived much worse. I could do this for her. We were friends. This was exactly what I agreed to.

"Great." She smiled. "By then, we'll almost be done. Make sure you call in whatever favors you need from me before you run out of time."

I turned to her. "I'm not passing so far?"

She shrugged. "You never know. I'm just reminding you."

This was not something I needed a reminder about. I felt every second pass. To me, things felt great. I enjoyed our daily texts, and she mentioned I was really improving in holding a conversation. She was going to start wearing my jersey to games. We were hanging out now. What else did I need to do?

Did Mitch have this same stress, or was he a normal person? I knew the answer, but that didn't explain why she didn't ask him to go to dinner with her friend.

"Why not Mitch?" I blurted.

She tilted her head, "Why not him, what?"

"Why didn't you ask him to go to the dinner with you?" I clarified.

She shrugged. "I guess I could have, but when Kerry and I were discussing it, you were the first person I thought of."

A tiny spark of pride flickered in my chest. "So you and him aren't…?"

She shook her head. "No, I told you. We're friends."

Right. It was stupid of me to keep pressing, but it was driving me crazy.

But why? What would it matter if they were dating? She and I were just friends. I should have been happy for her. Mitch was a great guy, and she deserved to be happy with whomever she chose.

I swallowed back the realization that was slowly creeping up.

It's because the thought of them together made me jealous. The name of that uncomfortable feeling tugging in my gut popped into my mind, and I couldn't deny it. I was jealous of Mitch.

I didn't have a logical reason to be, but that didn't make the feeling totally disappear. It felt like acknowledging the emotion breathed life into it. Now it was growing and taking up more and more room in my already cramped head. This was the last thing I needed to add to my life. I had more than enough stressors to drive me insane and keep me up at night.

"Parker?"

The sound of her voice pulled me back into reality. "Yeah?"

"I lost you there for a minute. Are you tired?"

I shook my head. "Sorry, just thinking."

"About what?" she asked while looking at her phone.

You. I wanted to say it but thought better of it. "I've just felt overwhelmed for the past few weeks, and it's starting to take it out of me."

"Is there anything you want to talk about?"

"Not really. I'm sure it will get better as I get more used to things here."

She smiled. "I think so too. Change as big as what you went through is a shock. Time will help, but I have an idea of what can make it better right now."

"What?"

"Food. Everything's so much better when you're not hungry." She waved her phone. "Delivery from wherever you want. Anything sound good?"

She had a point, but I didn't know of enough places to have a preference. "You choose."

"Hmmm." She pursed her lips, and after a second, I realized I was staring and looked away. "There's a really great deli with the best soups, sandwiches, and salads, or a place down the street that makes fresh stir-fry to order."

"Those both sound delicious." I stared up at the ceiling while deciding.

"Close your eyes," she directed.

I almost asked why but decided to just follow her instructions.

"Now focus on your mouth. Envision the food. What do you taste?"

Trying not to laugh, I closed my eyes, but food didn't appear in my mind. Her face with those lush lips coming closer. The slight blush in her cheeks as she looked up at me through her long lashes. I shook my head. I couldn't think about her like that. We were working on becoming friends. Nothing more.

I refocused my thoughts and decided a club sandwich was what I needed. Not the feel of her lips on mine.

I opened my eyes and grinned. "The deli."

"Perfect." She did a little happy dance-wiggle and tapped on her phone. "Tell me what you want."

After we ordered, she turned on the TV, and we settled next to each other to watch the evening news. Nothing particularly thrilling was going on in Salt Lake, but it was nice to be able to turn off my brain for a few minutes.

"Just so you know I was planning on watching a movie tonight, and since we're getting dinner now. You have to watch with me."

"What movie?"

She wouldn't look at me. "A good one."

"Oh, no."

She giggled, "It's really good. I promise."

"It's a chick-flick isn't it?"

"Yup."

I groaned. "fine."

"I'll consider letting you choose next time." She teased.

Minutes later, when she shifted and pulled a blanket from behind her to drape over her legs, she ended up even closer to me, close enough that I could feel the heat from her skin on mine and smell her floral shampoo. It shouldn't have caused a reaction in me. We weren't even touching, yet my whole body warmed, and I prayed she wouldn't look at me. I could only imagine how red and blotchy my face must be. I probably looked like I just spent a solid five minutes on the ice during a playoff game. At least I wasn't sweating. Yet.

That would be the cherry on top of this whole experience. I might be able to hide it for now, but once the food got here, I'd have to move.

I closed my eyes and focused on calming my breathing. I couldn't control most of my body's responses, but I could try my hardest to prevent this embarrassment from happening.

She laughed, and I flinched, opening my eyes, thinking she was laughing at me but she was watching the screen. Then Elena appeared on screen to cover the weather, and Viv perked up. "Oh, there she is!"

"I thought she did mornings."

"Me too." She paused. "Maybe she's having to cover for someone."

"Oh, right." That was the exact distraction I needed for my body to calm down. There was no reason to get so worked up. We were watching the news. Nothing unusual or romantic about that.

"What's your favorite movie genre?"

The question came from nowhere, but I answered automatically. "Action."

She shifted, her knee brushing up along my thigh. I felt the heat creeping back into my cheeks. "I should have guessed."

"What's yours?" I stared at her eyes, telling myself to ignore the fact that she was now, in fact, touching me.

"I like comedies and romances." She glanced away, to my relief, and I let out a breath. "What's your favorite food? Oh, and your favorite treat?"

Were we playing twenty questions now? "My mom's lasagna. I don't know what she does differently, if it's extra cheese or a special sauce, but I've never had one at a restaurant that comes close. And I love maple donuts."

Her eyes lit up when they met mine. "Really? That sounds amazing. You should get the lasagna recipe from her, and we can try to make it."

"Okay." I agreed. "What are yours?"

"Mine's close to yours. I love cheese and spinach ravioli." She bobbed her head. "My favorite treat is probably cookies-and-cream ice cream."

I gave an approving nod. "That's a solid choice."

"Most embarrassing moment?" She was grinning like a madwoman now.

"Ugh, do I have to?"

She chuckled. "As your best friend, it's something I need to know."

"Oh, we're best friends now?" I teased, feeling pretty proud of myself. I was getting more comfortable with her, and I liked it.

"Yes, I thought I made that clear earlier. You have to tell me."

I sighed. "Fine, I was eighteen, and my coach told me some scouts would be at the game. I got in my head and psyched myself out. I ended up missing passes, being way out of position, and basically screwed up the whole time. But the worst part was when I accidentally scored on my own team."

Her brows shot up. "That happens?"

"Not normally." I let out a chuckle. Something I couldn't

do for a long time. I'd been devastated back then. "It went viral, and I didn't live that down until I got traded to Anaheim."

She covered her mouth, but I could see the smile reach her eyes.

"It's okay. You can laugh."

That was all the permission she needed to burst out with uncontrolled laughter. "I can't believe it." She kept laughing until she sat straight up. "Is it still online?"

"No!" I reached across her for her phone. Her silky, soft hair tickled my arm as I snatched it away.

"Give me that! I need to see this!"

"No! You'll make it resurface and then the guys will see it and I'll suffer all over again."

She gave me a pretty solid attempt at puppy eyes. "Please?"

I shook my head and tucked the phone behind me. "Not a chance."

She leaned toward me, but the doorbell rang. She narrowed her eyes and pointed at me as she stood. "This isn't over."

I watched her answer the door and laughed. That woman knew how to keep me on my toes.

13

VIVIAN

P arker insisted on picking me up, and I realized why the second we walked out of the doors of my apartment building.

"Oh wow." I couldn't help but admire the beautiful car in front of me. I didn't know much about sports cars but this one looked fancy with electric blue paint and big gill-looking cutouts in front of the rear tires. "Is it fast?"

He grinned—a rare thing, I'd come to find out—and nodded. "Zero to sixty in three-point-two seconds."

I attempted an impressed whistle. "Very useful."

He chuckled and opened the door for me. It was like sitting on the ground, and I almost wished we could call a normal, human car so I didn't have to risk splitting my skirt open to climb in. The scent of new car was strong, and I ran my fingers over the buttery leather. This was nicer than any car I'd been in before. Including Jonathan and Simon's fancy high tech cars.

On the short drive to the restaurant, he showed me a few of the different features of the car. The screen greeted him by name, and he could change the colors of all the lights. Things

I never thought were necessary. "What do you drive?" he asked.

"I don't have a car," I replied.

You would have thought I told him I didn't believe in their existence by his shocked expression.

"Why?"

"I live two blocks from my office and within walking distance of everything else I need. If I do need to drive anywhere, Jess usually comes with me, or I use an app for a rideshare."

He stared forward at the street, waiting for the light to turn green. "Huh."

I laughed. "It's been about eight months, and I haven't minded. I actually like walking, as long as the weather isn't too bad."

"I admire you even trying." He glanced over at me for a split second. "I barely use mine, but I can't imagine not having the option."

"It was weird for the first few months, but I got used to it faster than I expected. I'm saving quite a bit from not having a payment, insurance, or paying for gas. Plus, parking can be a nightmare around here, so I don't have to worry about getting a ticket or not finding a spot."

Normally, when I got into a discussion about my radical decision with people, they understood the financial reasons more than just the health benefits. I wasn't sure that applied to professional athletes. The guys told me they generally didn't make as much as football, basketball, or baseball players, but they still made much more than the average person. I doubted saving a few hundred dollars a month was a big deal to any of them.

"Those are solid points. It's nice that you can do that here. Back in Anaheim, everything was too spread out."

"Oh, turn here." I pointed to the right, and he turned onto

the restaurant's street. He found a spot and told me to wait so he could open my door.

It was nice to have a hand help me out from so low. He effortlessly lifted me up, but maintaining my modesty was difficult. I'd have to remember to only wear pants when riding with him from now on.

"Thanks." I looked up at him to find him watching me with a smile.

"Of course."

We walked in side by side, almost touching but not quite. Kerry and AJ were waiting in the lobby, holding hands and looking even more in love than at the game.

"Hi, guys." I waved as we approached. "Nice to see you again," I said to AJ before twisting slightly to look up at Parker. "This is Parker."

Kerry must have prepared him since he just grinned and offered his hand. "Nice to meet you. I'm AJ."

"And this is Kerry," I told Parker while she stared at him with stars in her eyes. Evidently, it was her I needed to worry about, not her boyfriend.

"Ah, the other best friend," Parker said with a hint of teasing.

Kerry's eyes darted to mine. "Excuse me? When did he earn the title of *best*?"

I chuckled, and Parker put his arm over my shoulder. "When I gave her my jersey and let her watch one of the cheesiest rom-coms I've ever had the misfortune of seeing."

"It wasn't that bad," I protested, but he was right. It had been truly awful. I'd been willing to turn it off, but he said he was proving his dedication, so we both suffered through until the end.

"AJ, party of four?" The host called from the nearby stand.

"Here." AJ lifted a finger and we fell into line behind him.

The host eyed Parker for a second too long before turning and leading us to a booth toward the back of the restaurant. AJ went to the far side, so Parker and I would be facing away from the rest of the crowd. Did he do that on purpose? To give us more privacy? I appreciated the thought.

"Thanks, man," Parker said quietly as he lifted the menu.

AJ nodded once and slid his closer. "I know you're new here, but you're a pretty big deal already."

He was? I didn't follow sports news, or really local news for that matter, so I was fairly naive to how famous any of the guys from the team were. Did most people recognize him?

"I don't know about that." Parker ducked lower.

A week ago, I would have thought this was false modesty, but I knew him better now. He really didn't think he was a big deal. He was too shy to ever admit that. I was pretty sure if he could play hockey without any of the cameras, fans, or notoriety, he would. He was one of the few guys on the team that was a true introvert.

"So what's good here?" I asked, hoping to change the topic before Parker slid under the table and made a run for it. Kerry had asked if we had a preference for tonight, but I told her since Parker was new here and had been trying my usual picks to choose one of her favorites.

I'd been to this steakhouse once before, but it was a bit heavy for my taste. I didn't like leaving a meal feeling bloated and full to capacity.

"The steaks are all great, obviously, but I love their shrimp. It's served with the most delicious sauce," Kerry replied.

I scanned the options and found the grilled shrimp. "Sounds good."

"The ribeye is my favorite," AJ added.

"Oh, man. My mouth's watering," Parker said.

Our waiter came and didn't give our group a second glance. It was a strange feeling, studying everyone around us for reactions. Did Parker do this too, or was he used to it? I leaned over to ask at the same time he moved closer to me, making us nearly bump heads.

"Oh." I dipped back, and he grinned.

"Sorry, I was going to ask if you've had the sweet potatoes before. I'm not sure if I'd like the pecans," he asked in a whisper.

I shook my head. "I haven't." I read the description and shrugged. "It's probably good."

"I recommend the creamed spinach as well," AJ said.

Parker's face pinched in a disgusted frown behind his menu, and I had to bite my lip to keep from laughing.

By the time the waiter returned with our drinks, we managed to figure out what we wanted, and he disappeared swiftly once again.

"AJ, what do you do for a living?" I asked.

"I'm an accountant."

Well, there went the hope for that being a conversation point. It was one of the few jobs, much like mine, that no one ever asked follow-up questions about.

"That's impressive," Parker said, sounding completely genuine. "I'm horrible with numbers. I could never do what you do."

AJ's face lit up. "Same."

It only took one second before Parker burst out laughing. "Fair point. It's a good thing we all have different talents."

AJ laughed along with him, and Kerry beamed at me. I wasn't sure how this evening would go, but the guys seemed to be hitting it off. Maybe Parker didn't struggle with making new friends as much as he thought. He needed to give himself more credit.

"What do you do outside of work?" Parker asked.

"I'm a bit of a gamer," AJ admitted, looking slightly embarrassed.

"What do you play?" I asked.

"Some video games, but I have a group I play dungeons and dragons with every week. We've been getting together since our sophomore year of college," he answered.

"Wow. Really? That's awesome." Parker leaned forward. "Do you guys write any of your own campaigns?"

AJ shifted, sitting up straighter. "Yeah, we usually take turns."

"That's so cool. I played a bit back in high school with some kids on my team. We had to travel a lot on buses so that's how we passed the time."

I watched them discuss the game but couldn't participate. I knew nothing about it, but I was glad they had something to bond over.

Kerry caught my eye and raised a brow.

I smiled and mouthed, "I like him."

She grinned back. "Me too."

"Vivian, did you know much about hockey before meeting Parker?" AJ asked.

"A bit. My roommate is dating another guy on the team, so I've been going to games with her since December."

His brows rose, "Is that how you two met?"

Parker and I shared an amused look. "We were both helping my roommate set up for an event she planned the first time we met. Then the guys had a dinner party at my apartment, and we got to talk to each other a bit more there."

"And that's when I decided I wanted to be friends with her." Parker looked at me with true admiration in his eyes. "I watched her go from person to person, talking and laughing like it was the easiest thing in the world. I struggle with that, personally, so I really admired her. Then I noticed how much everyone liked her, and I decided I was obviously missing out, so I hunted her down and made her be my friend."

AJ laughed, but I spoke up. "He's not exaggerating. He really did."

"She is amazing," Kerry interrupted. "I'm glad you realized that so quickly."

"I have." Parker smiled at me, making my heart tingle with something unfamiliar. "She's the first person I've met that I don't feel like I have to try when I'm around her."

That was so similar to what Mitch told me. I never realized people saw me that way. I hoped to be seen as friendly and approachable, but this was the second time in a few days that it was so openly confirmed and by two reserved men. My heart threatened to burst with happiness.

As touched as I was, I didn't feel like I really knew Parker yet. He was private and very much lived in his head, but I wanted him to let me in. I wanted to know more about him. He'd answered every question I asked him the night we had dinner and watched that awful movie. Maybe that was the best way to get him to open up. I couldn't wait for him to start talking. I had to be direct.

"I feel that way about Kerry." AJ took her hand and kissed the back of it, making my friend blush bright red.

"Oh, stop," she gushed.

I peeked up at Parker, and he was smiling, watching them. Did he want that? A relationship? He never mentioned his dating life. That was another question I'd have to add to my growing list.

"Parker, where are you from?" Kerry asked.

"I was born and raised in Toronto, but once I got into the major juniors, I moved to Nova Scotia."

She nodded. "So is that where your parents live now?"

"No." His smile flickered. "I lived with a host family while I was there. My parents still live in Toronto."

"Really? How old were you when you moved?" AJ asked.

"Sixteen," he answered.

"Wow, that's so young." Kerry put her hand over her heart. "I don't think I could have done that."

"Me either," AJ agreed.

"I had a pretty good idea that was where my career was headed to the professional level, so I was prepared for it. I was lucky to make it onto a team."

My mind drifted to where I was at sixteen. An insecure, self-loathing girl that was lost and didn't have a plan or passion for anything. I was merely struggling to make it through each day. There was no way I could have made life-altering decisions at that age. His dedication matured him far beyond his years.

Even now, we were the same age, but he seemed far more experienced and seasoned in life.

"That's really amazing." I met his gaze. "I didn't even know what elective I wanted to take back then, let alone what I wanted to do with my life. I still don't."

He dropped his eyes. "I got lucky."

"That's only a small piece of it. You're also talented and disciplined and hardworking. There's no other way you could have made it this far."

He shrugged one shoulder.

He had every reason to be arrogant and stuck up, but he wasn't. It was so admirable. And with his blue eyes and easy smile combined with his shirt that was just tight enough to show off those well-earned muscles, he was undeniably attractive.

I cringed at the thought. I wasn't supposed to think of my best friend like that. We were platonic. I needed to remember that. I had to. Otherwise, I was going to end up hurt.

14

PARKER

V ivi invited me up to her apartment after dinner, and I quickly accepted. I wasn't ready to go home, and she was the only person I wanted to spend time with. I made myself comfortable on one end of the couch while she went to change.

"Ice cream?" she called as she appeared out of the hall in black sweats and a faded shirt with the Grand Canyon's outline of the front. She was twisting her long hair around on the top of her head, and in some sort of magic trick, she lowered her hands and the hair stayed in a messy bun.

"Is it cookies and cream?" I asked while trying not to stare at her. The length of her neck was exposed, and I had the sudden desire to trail my finger along the flushed skin.

"Are there other options?" she teased.

"In that case, yes please." I couldn't put my finger on exactly what it was about her that drew me in like never before. She'd dressed up tonight, and I'd seen her after work, looking polished and pretty. This was different. Truer.

"Is it weird for you to go out?" she asked while handing me a bowl of her favorite, cookies-and-cream ice cream. "I only caught one or two people staring, but I imagine it can get worse."

I poked the spoon against a chunk of black cookie, hoping she hadn't caught me watching her from across the room. Friends don't stare at each other. "Not usually. It's pretty rare that I get recognized. Hockey players generally aren't as well-known as other athletes, plus being new here means that most people haven't even heard my name yet."

"Is that what you prefer?" she asked while settling into the spot opposite me on the couch.

"Yeah. I can't imagine what it would be like to have strangers stop you on the street. I thought living with Mitch would expose me to that, but he said it rarely happens to him, and he's been here for a while."

"I don't think I would like that either. There would be too much pressure to always be on. You couldn't just leave the house like this"—she waved a hand down her body—"without someone spotting you. I'd hate to have a picture of that floating around the internet."

"I think you look great." The words slipped past my filter and were out there hanging between us like a bomb.

She lifted her head and grinned. "If you're aiming for a second helping, it's yours. You don't need to try to flatter me."

I swallowed. "I wasn't."

She laughed and placed a spoonful of ice cream in her mouth, then slowly pulled her spoon out with a satisfied smile. Her lips were so nice looking. Soft and plump.

What was happening to me? This was Vivi, my friend. I wasn't supposed to think of her like this.

Why was I fine when she was in a tight dress that showed off her curves in the best way possible, but the moment she appeared in sweats, I started losing my mind?

Would she let Mitch see her like this?

I doubted it. I wasn't sure where that thought came from, but it made my heart thump. She wasn't vain, but I'd never seen her without makeup and a coordinated outfit. Now, her eyes had smudges under her bottom lashes, and I noticed a mysterious stain on the left sleeve of her shirt.

She was letting me see her at her most relaxed. No pretenses or effort to show me the version of herself she shared with the world. This was her, in her home, being herself. That meant she was comfortable around me, right? My stomach tightened a bit.

I'd never been around a woman like this. They were always trying to impress me. Most of them were fake, pretending to be what they thought I wanted.

Vivi was never anything less than genuine. She was so different from every other woman I'd ever let into my life. Neither of us was trying to be something we weren't. I didn't strain myself to be more talkative or outgoing to please her. I didn't have to go to clubs and bars because it was where she expected me to be.

She let me be myself and accepted it. No manipulations or forcing me into the box of what she thought I should do or how I should act.

That was one of the lessons I learned on my last team. Most people had a very clear idea of what they thought a professional athlete should be. I usually let them down, so they tried to change me. I didn't resist because that would mean speaking up and possibly losing the few friends I had.

It was wrong. I knew that even in the moment, but I didn't fight it. It was easier to learn the lines and play the role.

The Fury wasn't that way. The guys didn't expect me to act a certain way or have one type of personality. They wanted me to be at my best and encouraged me to push myself, but it never crossed a line.

That was it.

That was how Viv made me feel too. Like it was okay to be me, quiet, unsure, and usually saying the wrong thing. She didn't mock me or make me feel less than. She was patient, giving me the extra time I needed to organize my thoughts or examine and understand my feelings before I responded to things.

With her, I didn't worry about my flaws or doubt myself.

"Are you listening?" she asked.

"No," I admitted. I'd been completely lost in my thoughts of her and didn't realize she'd spoken.

She slapped my knee. "Parker, I realized tonight that I don't really know *you*. I get you're more reserved, but I want to know what goes on inside that head of yours."

I nearly cringed. She really didn't want to know.

"Like what?"

"You mentioned your parents, but I don't even know if you have siblings."

Well, that was easy enough. "An older brother. He lives in Toronto too. He played hockey like most kids do but never really liked it. He's a math teacher now."

She leaned in. "Are you two close?"

I shrugged. "We text every few weeks, but we're both pretty busy."

"And your parents? Are you close to them?"

"I love my family, and wish we were closer, but since I moved out at sixteen I had to grow up fast. I've moved around a lot since then, and it's forced me to be independent. I guess that's why I tend to be quiet and kind of closed off. I didn't have a lot of opportunities to form lasting connections, like other kids in high school, so relationships are harder for me."

Her lips tipped up in a barely-there smile. "That makes a

lot of sense. You want to though, right? You want those relationships?"

I dropped my eyes and nodded. "It didn't bother me very much until I moved here. But yeah, now I do."

"Good, 'cause I think you're stuck with all of us for a while."

I chuckled. "I'm okay with that."

Her eyes sparkled as she laughed with me. "Me too."

"And what about you?" I asked, eager to know more about her. "I don't even know where you're from or anything about your family."

"I grew up in Arizona. My mom went to the university up here so that's why I chose it. I accidentally fell in love with the four seasons and the city, so I decided to stay. My parents still live just outside of Phoenix, and two of my three brothers stayed in the area. The oldest, Will, lives in Oregon."

"Three brothers? Wow." No wonder she could handle herself with all the guys on the team.

"Yeah, they're all older, too, so they loved to gang up on me and make sure I never forgot where I fell in the pecking order."

I let out a bark of laughter. "No wonder you're so tough."

She wrinkled her nose. "I don't think I'm very tough."

I just smiled. I thought that was the end, that I somehow lucked out with those easy questions, but she continued.

"So I know you don't have any hobbies, we've covered that, but what's your one thing. Like, what else do you like besides hockey?"

Since this question had come up over and over with the people here, I'd been thinking about it, trying to come up with a better response.

"The only thing I can think of is movies. I'm not really into who the director is, or the actors or anything like that, but when guys play video games on the plane, I watch movies."

She perked up. "Okay, so what's your favorite? I know you like action, but specifically, what's your favorite movie or series?"

"The Marvel Universe."

She paused. "Like the superhero movies?"

I nodded.

She eyed me, lips pursed, and finally answered. "I haven't ever seen a full one."

I hesitated, finally stunned by something about her. "Any of them?"

She shook her head. "I've seen bits and pieces, but I've never sat down to watch one of them."

"How have you managed to avoid them for so long?" It seemed impossible.

"I haven't really tried. I tend to only have girlfriends, and when the option of going to the movies comes up, we choose something else."

It didn't make sense she could watch terrible romantic comedies that had no plot, but had never seen even one of the well-done films from the Marvel Universe. "There are so many, and they've been coming out for over a decade. How could you not see even one?"

She shrugged, almost laughing. "I'm sorry to have offended you."

I opened my mouth, then snapped it closed. "We're watching them."

She narrowed her eyes. "All of them?"

I started looking for the remote. "Starting now."

"But..." She paused, then shook her head. "Should we watch *Thor* or *Iron Man*?"

I stared at her. "You can't just jump in wherever you want.

We're watching *Captain America*. We'll work through them chronologically." I took a big bite of my melting ice cream.

"I didn't realize there were rules." She picked up the remote and selected the movie.

"We're doing this right," I said. "And we're not stopping until you've seen them all."

She laughed. "Fine."

I didn't mention that there were twenty-three, so far. There was no way we'd finish in a in the next few days, so she unknowingly extended our friendship by several months. I'd keep that information to myself for now.

Before the opening credits were done, she reached forward to put her empty bowl on the coffee table, then pulled a gray and teal blanket from off the arm of the couch and draped it over her legs.

I finished and placed my bowl next to hers before settling back. There was about a foot of empty space between us and I wanted to shift closer, but I wasn't sure how. The memory of the feeling of her so close to me the last time we'd been here wouldn't fade, and I craved her heat touching me.

I was losing myself. I put my hands in my lap and focused on the movie, but I knew it line for line, so it wasn't an adequate distraction. She was right there. All I had to do was spread my legs out a bit more and our knees would touch. No, that would be unnaturally wide. She'd know I wasn't sitting normally.

But would that be enough? Just some knee contact? If anything, it would only intensify the urge.

Pretending like nothing was going on was like having an intense itch I couldn't scratch.

This was worse than when I was thirteen and at my first boy and girl birthday party. I hadn't known how to act then, and now twelve years later, I was no better off.

How could she be so comfortable with me, yet I couldn't bring myself to physically move closer to her?

It wasn't like I wanted to put my arm over her shoulder and sneak a kiss. No, that was too far.

I wouldn't really mind kissing her. The image of her lips on the spoon returned, and I nearly groaned.

"Are you cold?" Vivi asked. Before I could respond, she held up the blanket and patted the spot right next to her. "We can share."

I looked at where her hand lay and blinked. Right there.

Yes. I could do that.

"Thanks." I scooted over, but she wasn't satisfied.

"Come on, I won't bite." She met me in the middle, lining up our legs and arms so we touched from her shoulder to her ankle. The suddenness of it all made me still while she carefully spread the blanket out to cover both of us. "You can use the coffee table."

She kicked one foot up and used it to drag the table a few inches closer so she could use it as a footrest. I did the same after toeing off my shoes under the table. She left her foot resting against mine, and I stared at the contrast of my plain black socks to her rainbow fuzzy ones. Once she was content, she sighed and her body seemed to melt against me.

I closed my eyes for a second, thanking the universe for ending my agony before the feel of her registered and a new form of torture began.

This was what it was like to be so close to something, or someone, you couldn't have. Like a steak dangling before a lion, just out of reach.

Vivi was my friend. She trusted me to maintain that relationship. I refused to ruin that. Even if it was so, so tempting.

15

VIVIAN

"You're looking dashing this fine morning," Kerry teased as she appeared in front of my desk with two steaming mugs. She offered one to me, and I greedily accepted it before taking a big gulp while she looked over my messy bun and wrinkled shirt.

"It's a good thing you came bearing gifts. I'll choose to ignore your insult." I covered my mouth as another yawn escaped.

"What, or should I say *who*, kept you up so late?" She dragged a chair over and sat across from me.

"You know I was at the game." I took another sip of coffee waiting for the caffeine to hit my bloodstream.

"A game that ended around nine. Plenty of time for you to get home and get a full night's rest in."

I yawned again. "Jess was driving, and everyone wanted to go out to celebrate again."

"So you got home at what? Ten? Ten-thirty?"

I narrowed my eyes, "Since when did you become my mother?"

She grinned. "So, what happened?"

"Nothing." I took another sip. "We went to dinner, ate, and got home around eleven."

"We who?"

"Me and Jess," I replied blandly.

"And what about Parker?" She finally got to her point.

"What about him?"

"How did he respond to seeing you in his jersey?" She wagged her brow.

I cringed. "How do you manage to make that sound dirty?"

She shrugged. "A gift."

I rolled my eyes. At least our bosses were out this morning at an off-site meeting, so there was no one to catch us chatting.

"He said he liked seeing his number."

"On you," she guessed.

"Yes, that might have been mentioned specifically." I could feel my cheeks warming and tried to hide behind my mug.

She jabbed her finger in my face. "I knew it."

"Knew what?" I asked in a bored tone even though I'd been dying to have this conversation with her since we said goodbye at the restaurant last night.

The few texts Kerry and I had exchanged over the weekend were mostly me assuring her I liked AJ and that Parker had really said he had a good time.

"You like him," she said in a singsong voice.

"I don't," I protested while looking around for any eaves-droppers. We were alone, so I calmed a bit.

"You do. AJ and I were talking about it. He asked me right when we got in the car. He was all, 'I thought you said they were just friends. It didn't look that way to me.'" She raised her brows. "And I said I was just as surprised as him because, from everything you've said, you two are just friends but now we know that's a load of rubbish."

"We *are* just friends, Kerry." I might as well have been shouting at a wall.

"I saw it the moment you guys walked in. You weren't holding hands, but you were standing so close to each other. I could practically feel the sparks shooting off between you two." She sighed. "And don't get me started on the way he looks at you."

"What are you talking about?" I tried to sound indignant, but I was curious now.

"His eyes sparkle when he looks at you. And he gets this tiny smile when you talk. It's like the corners of his lips lift without him realizing it."

That sounded so sweet. And romantic. And not at all like reality.

"Kerry, he is just my friend. I'm pretty sure that's just how his face looks."

She barked out a laugh. "Oh, no. Don't try to talk yourself out of this. I know what I saw, and I'm not the only one. AJ will back me up. There is something between the two of you, whether or not you want to admit it."

I didn't.

She wasn't wrong, at least she wasn't wrong about me. I did feel something more than friendship toward Parker, especially after this weekend. He only told me a bit about how he grew up, but it made me understand him so much better. I could feel how important it was to him to have someone he could talk to, someone he could establish a relationship with. He needed to know there was someone who cared about him and knew him. I wanted to be that person more than anything.

And the spark she swore she saw? Yeah, I felt that anytime we were close.

It was like a rope tugging us together. When we were on

the couch before *Captain America* started, I knew I couldn't stand to sit there next to him, but just out of reach. I wouldn't have been able to watch the movie, let alone retain any of it, and I knew he'd ask me questions when it was over. Did I use an incredibly lame excuse to share a blanket just so I could snuggle into him? Yes, I did. But it worked. He seemed to relax too. It only took a few minutes for him to relax against me, and I even used his arm as a pillow when I got tired halfway in. It was a very nice arm. Solid, but not so hard that it was uncomfortable. I gave it four well-deserved stars.

Being close to him, but not quite close enough, was like losing or forgetting your phone. It's uncomfortable, distracting, and something you'd do pretty much anything to remedy as fast as possible.

I wanted to hug him when he was leaving but didn't know if that was a step he was ready for. A cuddle of convenience was different from a direct, intentional contact. When he didn't even pause after pulling on his coat before reaching for the door, I had my answer. He didn't want a hug. Or anything more.

"I can't," I finally said.

"Why not?" She leaned forward, resting her elbow on the desk and putting her chin in her palm.

"Because," I started and immediately ran out of words. How could I say this so she would understand? "Because we agreed to be friends."

"So?"

I sighed. "Feeling anything else is going against the agreement."

"Why is that a bad thing?" A small grin slipped from her lips before she caught herself.

"We've managed to actually open up to each other. We're getting more comfortable and really starting a relationship.

That's big for him and for me. I don't want to ruin this with feelings." I whispered the last word.

"Why do you think that would ruin anything? Telling him how you feel might just deepen the relationship, make it better."

Yes, there was that possibility, but more likely was the reality that my feelings would be one-sided. That whatever Kerry thought she saw from him was her bias as my best friend tainting things. She wanted Parker to like me, so she saw it. There's some psychology behind that, I was sure.

"This is a good thing," I said. "There's more to life than love and romance. Maybe what we both need is someone to rely on. Someone he feels comfortable opening up to and being himself around and someone that I can trust to like me for me."

She pursed her lips. "Everyone likes you for you, Viv."

I shrugged. "Maybe now, but it hasn't always been like that. I'm used to people wanting to be friends with me to get to someone else, especially men. This is the first relationship I've ever had with a man, even if it is platonic, without having to worry about figuring out what he's really after. I didn't realize how badly I wanted that until now." I blew out a breath. "I don't want to give that up."

"I get that, but it's my duty as your best friend to make sure you're not getting in your own way. I don't want you to miss out on something amazing because you're afraid."

"I'm not afraid," I argued.

She gave me a stern look. "You are. You're afraid of putting yourself out there and risking rejection. You're afraid of being happy. Of wanting more than what you have now. I get it though. I can't make you ready when you're not, so for now, I'll let it slide. But if I need to, I won't hesitate to kick your butt for your own sake."

I chuckled. "I know you will." But she wouldn't have to because I knew I was right.

"Good." She blew me a kiss and stood up. On her way to her side of the office, I heard her singing, "Sitting in a tree, k-i-s-s-i-n-g."

It was a good thing my boss wasn't around because I could not bring myself to focus. Kerry's words repeated in my mind like a bad pop song. She really thought she saw something from Parker? It wasn't much of a guess for her to pick up on my attraction. She knew me well enough to see that I had developed more complicated and confusing feelings toward him. I didn't even know how to hide that from her.

But no, she said Parker's eyes sparkled when he looked at me, and he had a special smile when I spoke?

Ugh. Things like that went straight to my head. What did it mean?

I pretended to be updating a budget spreadsheet while really mulling over that question. Was there a chance he felt more than friendship for me? Could he really be attracted to me?

Then again, this was all new for him. Maybe he was fascinated by me. Maybe that was how he looked at all his real friends.

Kerry was the worst. I never should have let her sit down. I could have taken the coffee and told her I was too busy to talk. I saw the look on her face. I should have known better.

Stupid me for thinking she wanted to discuss AJ. Oh no. She barely even mentioned him. That would have been concerning, but it proved to me that her feelings for him were real and rooted and not something she needed to analyze with me. She knew how she felt, and he probably did too.

Lucky jerks. Must be nice to have it so easy. It was clear

to them from the beginning. That was one of the benefits of meeting on an app. You already knew that both parties were interested in a relationship and that they found the other person attractive. No second-guessing there.

Meanwhile, I was in the grayest of gray, murky water. Nothing was clear. I wasn't even sure where I was going. The safest thing to do was simply paddle still and wait for rescue.

Did that mean Parker? Waiting on him?

What if that took years? Decades? I sincerely doubted he would ever make the first move. He probably didn't even know it was something that he had to do.

It would come down to me. I would have to be the one to say something. To even bring up the topic of there being something growing between us.

I really, really didn't want to have to do that.

The burden of laying myself bare and risking rejection felt impossible. Too overwhelming to even consider.

Kerry was right. I was afraid. Terrified. Petrified. Frozen in fear.

I sucked in a deep breath. Nothing had to be decided right away. Things were new. Our friendship was working. A budding friendship was good. I was happy with how things were going, so there was no urgent need to tell him.

I wasn't even sure my feelings were real. It could just be the novelty of having a new guy in my life. I'd wait to see if they disappeared before saying anything. This could all be a fleeting crush. I slumped a bit. Yeah, it wasn't anything to stress about.

In fact, I could test it. I could find a new man to go out with. A real date to see if I was interested in someone else, anyone else. Maybe Mitch had a friend he could set me up with. A trial run. Since Parker and I were just friends, there wasn't anything wrong with going on a date with another guy.

The more I thought about it, the better it sounded. Plus, when I told Parker about the date, I could watch for a reaction from him. That would tell me how he felt about me. Maybe.

No. This was a solid plan. Mission: Get a Date was a go.

16

PARKER

E ven though we lived together, I rarely saw Mitch outside of practice and games. I wasn't sure what his schedule was, but he was almost never home. He did appear right before practice to see if I wanted to carpool, but I never knew where he was coming from, if it was the boxing gym or some other secret hang out.

His lack of communication was fine with me. I didn't necessarily want to have to check in with anyone either. But it was odd. I still felt like a visitor in his apartment. At one point, I thought he might be giving me space to settle in, but that wasn't working out for me. Being alone in his home made me more uncomfortable with each passing day. It was probably time to look into getting my own place.

Maybe after practice today, I'd ask the guys for advice. There was a chance one of them knew of an opening in their apartment building. As much as I didn't want to offend Mitch, I was sure the space would be best for both of us.

I was checking my bag to make sure I had a change of clothes when he appeared in my doorway.

"Hey, do you mind driving today?" he asked.

"Sure." I zipped my duffle and pulled the strap over my shoulder. "Are you ready?"

"Yeah."

We headed to the front door, and he grabbed his bag from the couch. Normally, the silence between us didn't bother me, but there was something eating at me, and there was no way of knowing when I'd have another chance to talk to him. The short drive to the arena was the perfect amount of time. If things got awkward, we'd have an excuse to avoid each other for the next few hours.

He pushed the button to call the elevator and stepped back next to me.

This was it. I just needed to open my mouth.

I swallowed. "You're close with Vivian."

He twisted his neck to face me so fast I thought it was going to crack. "Yeah?"

"How close exactly?" I could only meet his eyes for a second before looking away.

"I'm not sure what you mean."

The bell dinged, and we stepped into the elevator. I pressed the button for the garage. "You two are friends."

"Yeah, Parker. We've established that." He shifted from one foot to another. "What about it?"

"You took her to dinner a few weeks ago."

He blew out a breath. "Yup."

"And you were at her apartment the other night." I wasn't sure why I was repeating facts he was well aware of. I just needed to lay out all I knew to make sure I had all the right pieces.

"Parker, what are you getting at?" He turned to face me, but the doors opened and I hurried out.

I didn't say anything until we got to my car. I looked at him, pausing with my hand on the roof. "Is there anything else going on?"

He stared at me for a long moment before cracking a smile. "You mean, more than friendship?"

I nodded.

"No, she and I are just friends."

I opened the door and slid inside, and he did the same. I went through the motions of starting the car, letting it warm up, and pulling out of the spot.

"Is there a reason why you're asking?"

I glanced over, expecting him to be smiling. It sounded like he was teasing me, but he looked serious.

"I just wanted to check."

"Why?" he pressed.

I turned onto the street and crossed the four lanes to the left turn lane, focusing so much on the traffic, hoping he'd let it go. I got the information I was after, and was relieved to be able to know where he stood. I didn't expect him to keep pressing me.

"Because I'm also her friend."

I could see him watching me out of the corner of my eye.

"And you want to be her only friend?"

I shook my head. "No, of course not. I'm glad you two are friends."

He chuckled. "Oh man. You've got it bad."

I met his gaze and quickly looked away. "I don't know what you're talking about."

"Yes, you do," he countered.

"She and I are just friends," I clarified, for both of us.

"But you wish you were more."

I closed my eyes and took a deep breath. The realization that struck me the night at her place--that I might actually feel something more than friendship for Vivi--was something I wished I could squash and forget about for a while, but that wasn't how things like this worked.

There was too much at stake. At least, that's how it felt to me. I wasn't willing to lose the connection I had with her just because I had more feelings for her than I expected. She was the first person in my life, in years, if ever, that simply saw me as I was. She didn't try to change me to meet the expectations she had in her mind of who or what I should be. She didn't see me as just a hockey player. I wasn't some novelty to brag about. She made sure I was comfortable whenever we were together. She cared. She thought about me before herself.

Maybe that was just friendship, but it didn't feel like that.

The desire to be near her was driving me crazier each day. It was like my body and mind craved her. The peace she brought me. The gentle way she pushed me without ever expecting anything, like when she invited me to dinner with her friends. She noticed the looks but didn't play into the attention as other women had before. She didn't want to be seen with me for some sort of notoriety. She was perfectly content hanging out on her couch, watching my favorite movies. It was me that wanted to step outside of my comfort zone for her. I wanted to take her out and show her off. I wanted her to wear my jersey so people knew she was with me. It was silly. Juvenile even, but she brought that out in me. She made it okay for me to not be so serious. To open up and laugh and joke. She gave me a break from the daily pressures of my career.

With her, we were just Vivi and Parker.

"Yeah, I think so."

He bumped his elbow into mine. "Good."

"Good?" I repeated. "Why is that good?"

"Because I really like her. I'm going to be protective of her, no matter what, because she's one of the rare ones. She's sweet and honest and real in a way that's hard for guys like us to find. But I also like you. I think you both have something to offer the other, a way to better each other. That's what relationships are meant to do. Not change the other person, but lift each other up. Together."

That was more than I expected him to say. It might have been the most he'd ever said to me, but every word pierced my heart.

"That's how I see her." It was shocking how well he understood us. Me.

"I know. That's why I think you should tell her how you feel."

I turned into the parking lot and waved at the guard. "You really think so?"

"Yes," he answered simply.

"What if she doesn't feel the same? We agreed to be friends, and I really like how things are now. I don't want to ruin that."

He grinned. "You'll never know for certain until you try. She's the only one that can tell you how she feels, but I have a good feeling about it."

He was friends with her, so maybe he knew something I didn't. Or just understood her well enough to guess.

"Come on, if we're late, we'll be stuck doing drill lines for an extra hour." He got out of the car like things were completely normal.

I climbed out and reached for my bag, feeling off-kilter. I was all mixed up. While I had a sense of relief that Mitch didn't also have feelings for Vivi, I was now weighed down by the pressure of acting on this information.

Nothing had to happen now. That was the only peace I had. I didn't need to go running off to find her to admit my feelings this moment. I didn't even need to do anything for the next week, or longer. There was no rush.

We could take things slow. Continue to get to know each other and gradually let things naturally evolve. One day, the progression would lead to us being more than friends.

"Come on, I know you're thinking about her, but you've got to focus for the next few hours. Your crush will be there after practice." Mitch chuckled, and I shook my head and followed him over to the elevators where Schultz and Murray were already waiting.

"Hey," Mitch greeted as we joined them.

"Oh, hey. Can you guys help settle a debate?" Schultz asked.

Murray groaned. "Don't involve more people."

His brother-in-law ignored him and turned to us. "As each other's only family, Chloe and I have to look out for one another."

Murray shook his head. "I've never argued that."

"In the case of an emergency, I should be able to help her, right?" Schultz asked us.

I shrugged. "Yeah, I guess."

Mitch narrowed his eyes. "What specifically do you mean?"

"See, even he knows you're up to something," Murray grumbled and held the elevator door open for us all to get in.

"Reesey-boy won't let me have the key or garage code to their house. Even though I'm family and live less than three minutes away. If there ever were an emergency, I could get there faster than any first responders. I should be able to get to my sister and nephew if needed."

I began nodding, but Murray held up a finger. "Oh no. Don't twist the story for them. *Madi* has a key and the code. If something ever happens or we need you to get in the house, she can."

"What if she's not around, and I still need to get in?" Schultz argued.

"Dude, it's not going to happen. Stop harassing me and

your sister. I swear, if Callan was old enough, you'd be pressuring him too."

"He'd give it to me. He loves his uncle," Schultz pouted. "Why can't I have a key?"

"Because you will use it for evil!" Murray shouted and pushed his way past us to the locker room.

"I would never!" Schultz called after him.

Murray spun around. "You already have! You broke in and disconnected our water heater. We had to take cold showers for three days until a plumber could come. Your nephew suffered."

Schultz shrugged. "He and Chloe came over to our house. It was really only you that suffered."

Mitch and I shared a look. I wanted to laugh, but I was too scared of Murray to let it out.

"Then, you snuck in and put buckets of water above every door so we got drenched, and you ruined the hardwood in my office and the hallway."

"That was an unfortunate consequence. One I paid for!" Schultz threw up his hands. "That was months ago. I've matured!"

"No, you haven't. I will never give you free access to my house." Murray walked away without waiting for a response.

"He's such a killjoy. I swear he doesn't have a funny bone in his body." Schultz sighed and followed after him.

"Are they always like that?" I asked.

This was the first time I'd been on a team with people who were related, even by marriage.

"Pretty much, yeah. They're driving each other crazy every chance they get. Mostly Schultz pushing Murray's limits. I'm pretty sure the reason the team hasn't separated them is because they work so well together on the ice. I think their closeness makes it easier for them to predict one another's movements, and I swear they can read each other's minds."

From what I'd seen, even before I moved here, that was true. They had a dynamic that couldn't be manufactured. It was completely natural, which likely meant they'd stay together for their careers, even if it drove Murray crazy.

At least it was entertaining for the rest of us, and it distracted Mitch from pressing me about Viv.

17

VIVIAN

Mitch didn't reply to my text until minutes before I was leaving the office for the day. He said he was home and available, so I called him.

"Hey, Vivi," he answered.

"Hi, I have something to ask you, but I'd rather do it in person." So I could see the reaction on his face.

"Oh sounds intriguing."

I chuckled at his teasing tone. "Can you meet somewhere?"

"You don't want to come over?" he asked.

"It's something I'd rather not have your roommate overhear."

He hummed. "Well, Parker isn't here right now. He stayed late at practice with his line."

"Do you know how long he'll be?" The last thing I wanted was for him to walk in during this conversation.

"Usually another hour or two. If you want to play it safe, we can meet at a cafe or restaurant if you're hungry."

I was too nervous to eat, but maybe a soothing tea could

help. "There's a cafe a few blocks from my office. I'll send you the address."

"Okay, I'll meet you there."

I found the website and sent it to him before shutting down my laptop and making sure everything important was locked in my desk before leaving. It was only a ten-minute walk for me, but he was waiting near the doors when I entered.

"Hey." He stepped forward and gave me a warm hug.

"Hi." I smiled up at him. "Have you been here before?"

"Yeah, a few times." He looked around like he expected to see someone, then stepped forward to join the line.

We ordered our drink, and he paid, despite my attempts to give my card to the barista. He guided me to a pair of oversized chairs in the back corner. "Is this okay?"

I glanced around the nearly-empty room. We'd arrived between the lunch and evening crowd so we didn't have to worry about being overheard or rushed for our seats. "Perfect."

"So tell me, what's going on?" He sat back with his foot resting on the opposite knee.

"Right to it? We're not even going to go through the normal small talk?" I asked, only half-joking.

"This sounded really important. I didn't think you wanted to waste time on pleasantries, but if it makes you feel better. I'm fine. Sore, but that's nothing new. How are you?"

I attempted to smile but it fell short. "I'm stressed."

"Okay, why is that?"

I scooted back in the worn leather, trying to get comfortable.

"Here are your drinks," a female voice announced behind me. She set our drinks down and left without another word. I reached for my tea and removed the lid to blow on the steaming liquid.

"We can talk while it cools down." Mitch shot me a knowing look.

Okay, maybe I was procrastinating. My determination to get this done was dwindling now that he was in front of me.

"I was wondering," I began, and he watched patiently. "If you have any friends."

His lips quirked. "I'm lucky enough to have a few, yes."

I dropped my head. This was so much harder than I thought. "No, that's not what I meant."

"I hope not," he countered and took a sip of his tea.

"Do you have any friends that you would be willing to set me up with?" I rushed out the words and then dropped my eyes to my drink. This was stupid. I couldn't bring myself to see his reaction. I didn't want to know anymore.

He coughed, choking on his drink.

"Oh no!" I stood and offered him some napkins as if that was at all useful to him.

He waved me off and calmed down enough to breathe normally. "Sorry, that's just not what I was expecting to come out of your mouth."

"Why not?" I was a single woman. He likely had single friends. It was pretty normal, as far as I knew, to ask your friends to set you up. At least, Kerry thought it was when I ran the idea past her. I didn't mention any details. Just if it would be okay to ask a friend and if it would if it would make her feel like I was taking advantage of her, but she was encouraging. She said it was completely different than using someone. Besides dating apps, how else were you supposed to meet people?

"Because," he paused. "I thought there was something going on between you and Parker."

I shot back, "What? No. We're just friends."

He glanced down and nodded. "Right, my bad."

"Why do you think there's something going on between us?" Yes, I was letting my insecurity get the best of me. I wanted to hear someone else confirm that maybe this wasn't all in my head.

"I've seen you two together. From when you first met to now, there's a big difference. You're really comfortable around each other. I've seen the looks and little innocent touches that seem to happen at every opportunity. It's like you two gravitate toward one another."

I didn't think anyone else, outside of Kerry and maybe Jess, had noticed there was anything going on. Apparently, we weren't as discrete as we thought.

"It's all platonic." I wasn't sure who I was trying to convince, him or me.

"If you say so." He watched me over his mug as he sipped.

It felt like he was peering into my soul, like he could tell I was lying.

"It started out that way," I admitted. "We only ever intended on being friends, but I think I might have a little crush."

He lowered his mug, revealing a smile. "But you want to go out with someone else?"

"I have to. I need to figure out if what I'm feeling is just the novelty of having a new guy around that's nice to me and gives me attention, or if there's something real between us."

He didn't say anything for a long while, then finally conceded. "Okay."

"So, can you think of anyone?" My confidence in this whole plan was quickly diminishing. What was I thinking? This was stupid. If I really wanted to figure out if my feelings for Parker were genuine, there better ways to go about it.

"A few," he admitted, though it didn't sound like he

wanted to. "There are one or two guys from my boxing gym I can think of that would love the opportunity to go out with a woman like you, but I'm not sure I want them to."

My shoulders slumped. "Why not?"

"Because you're too good for them." He shot me a look. "My barber might be a good choice too." He stared down at his drink. "Are you sure you really want this?"

"Yes." I tried to not leave any doubt in my voice. I had to do this. It was the fastest way to either get Parker out of my system or know for certain my feelings were real. "I'm not looking for a relationship, Mitch. I just want to see who's out there. I haven't dated in a while, and I think it's time to try."

"How long is a while?" he asked.

I pretended to have to think about it, but I knew exactly when my last disastrous experience had been. "A little over a year."

He blew out a long whistle. "Why?"

Because some men sucked and could break your heart with a few choice words. "My last relationship ended badly, and I decided to take some time to focus on myself."

"Fair enough, I can't really judge. I haven't been on a date in about eight months."

This sounded intriguing. "What happened?"

"He didn't like being with someone prettier than him." He winked.

I shook my head. There was something bigger, but if he didn't want to tell me, I understood. It wasn't like I shared my whole truth.

"Then maybe we should make it a double date," I suggested.

"You've got some ideas for me?"

There were a few men at the office that I knew were out, but I didn't know them well enough to know if they would be a good fit for Mitch. I didn't want to be the one to push him even further into singlehood.

"Not exactly, but give me some time, and I could come up with a solid option."

He waved me off. "I don't have time for dating right now. Playoffs are coming up."

I narrowed my eyes. I happened to know that the playoffs were months away, but I let it go. I knew what it was like to not be ready and how annoying it was when people tried to push you.

"Fine. But once off-season starts, all bets are off."

"Sure." He chuckled. "Let me think about it and feel out the guys. I'll let you know in a day or two if I have any leads."

"Thanks." I hadn't expected to be so nervous, but now, everything was out in the open and I got it all off my chest. I wasn't alone in this anymore. Bringing in Mitch, Parker's roommate and teammate, was a risk, but I trusted him.

"You know it's okay if you really do have feelings for Parker."

I set my drink down. "What do you mean?"

"I get that it's probably scary to acknowledge it, but you can't let fear hold you back. You're my friend and I care about you, so I wouldn't say this if I didn't mean it, but he's a good guy. I've seen him bust his butt to prove himself to the team. He's gone above and beyond what anyone expects from him, and I'm not the only one that's noticed. The other guys are really impressed, and that takes a lot." He stretched and switched his legs, resting his hand on his knee. "I know that's mostly based on his attitude and actions on the ice, but that translates to who he is as a person. It's okay to be attracted to that."

My throat was so thick I had to take several gulps of tea before I felt like I could speak. I hadn't expected Mitch to praise Parker like that. It wasn't something he needed to do, but his words confirmed who I believed Parker to be. It was comforting but also stung. He was a really good person. And so handsome. And talented. And honest.

Why would I think I deserved him when I was going behind his back and trying to date someone else?

Because it was a test. It was the only way I knew how to make certain of how I felt.

"You think I'm making a mistake." I whispered the words, not sure I wanted the answer.

"I think you're doing what you think you need to do. No one can tell you if that's a mistake. It's not like you're cheating on him. You're just exploring your options as a single woman. There's nothing wrong with that."

I sighed. "I could be worrying over nothing. I could go on a date and realize that I am really falling for him and it might not matter. I'm only one-half of the equation. I could end up going through this just to find out he doesn't feel the same."

The thought made me feel ill, even if it was what I expected to happen.

"You owe it to both of you to see." Mitch's voice sounded a million miles away.

"No, this is all a mistake. I should stop now. I should just let things be." I looked up and met his worried eyes. "Things are good. We're good. I'm happy, and I think he is too. Why mess that up?"

"Vivi, that's fear talking. You can't let that dictate your life. Think of all you'd miss out on if you were scared and never pushed yourself. Would you have gone to college? Moved away from your parents? Started your job? Let a stranger move into your apartment? Talk to me?"

I narrowed my eyes at the last one. "You think I was afraid of you?"

"You called me a highlander. Aren't those men intimidating?"

I almost laughed but fell short. "I am scared, Mitch."

"It sounds to me like you're about to do something big."

Yeah, a big mistake.

18

PARKER

W e only had tonight's game left before a week of traveling. It was another change, another new experience, to get anxious about. It wasn't the traveling that was the issue, it was doing it the first time with a new team. Coming in during the middle of the season had a dozen negatives, but trying to stay out of the way and not messing up the established flow was one of the hardest. Navigating my way through the unwritten rules and my teammates' habits should have come with an instruction manual, but the best I had was Mitch, and maybe Jason and Brandon, to give me a heads up.

But I couldn't worry about that until tomorrow. We had a game to win before that. I didn't need any of the guys to point out the Pride's section to me tonight. My eyes found them without thinking, and I zeroed in on Vivi, smiling at her and offering a nod when she caught me staring.

She was wearing my jersey again.

It felt good. There was something about knowing that at least one person cared about me in the arena of fans that didn't trust me yet. It took time to earn their respect, and I'd get there one day, but all that mattered to me was her.

She was here with Jess and the other women and probably came to hang out with them, but I let myself think I was another reason. She was cheering for me.

I was determined to make her proud to be wearing my number.

"Vivi asked for mine." Mitch scooted closer to me on the bench. "I told her I'd get it to her in time for the next game."

"What are you talking about?" I asked.

"My jersey. She said she wanted to support all her friends."

I refused to look at him. He was doing this on purpose. I never should have admitted my feelings. I gave him the perfect ammo and expected him to what? Leave it alone?

This was my mistake. I should have known there would be consequences. Heckling was the first.

"I'm her friend, should I get her one of mine too?" Jake asked from next to Mitch.

I would not give them the satisfaction of rattling me. She could rotate through the entire team. It didn't matter, I knew who she was really here for.

"Yeah, and we might as well get Lance and Mikey's too," Mitch added.

"Hey, what about me? We're friends," Jason said from my left.

"Don't forget me," Derek called from the chair in front of the door. How had he even heard this conversation?

"Nah, she wants to wear the jerseys of players that actually step on the ice," Brandon countered.

I cracked a smile, but I didn't speak.

"Hey, shut up and focus," Schultz shouted from down the line. "And if she needs a jersey to wear, she's going to wear the star's."

"Yeah, mine," Murray said with a grin.

"All of you stop. Now." Hartman leaned forward and locked eyes with each of us. "She'll wear mine. Now get ready." He nodded and I stood with Jason and Brandon.

"Twenty bucks she wears mine before yours," Schultz said to Murray who bumped his glove in agreement.

I shook my head, threw my leg over the boards, and left their taunts on the bench. I had one job to do, and I wasn't going to let them get to me.

"Here!" Jason slapped his stick on the ice as we crossed through the neutral zone, and I got in position, waiting for Brandon to pass.

It was a play we'd been practicing every night for a week and finally felt ready to try out. The puck shot toward me, and I adjusted my weight so I could backhand it to Jason. He was ready, and we'd moved quicker than our opponents could keep up with. Brandon was ready for a rebound, but it wasn't necessary. Jason's shot was perfect, just over the goalie's right shoulder. We scored, pulling ahead by three points. A comfortable lead for the third period.

"Yes!" Jason and Brandon crashed into me with Jake and Lance.

Jason led us to the bench, bumping gloves with the team as we skated past before taking our seats.

"Well done," Hartman called before he pushed away from the boards with the first line.

Jason, Brandon, and I continued getting slaps and congratulations while the game continued. I looked for Vivi and saw her and Taylor jumping up and down together, still celebrating our goal.

She didn't do that when Murray, Koslov, or Hartman scored. Just me, well my assist. The details didn't matter. She was cheering for me. She came to see me. The pride that filled me was borderline primal. Like the Neanderthal within took her clapping as claiming me.

Maybe that's what I wanted. To be able to call her mine. Not in a possessive way, but with the knowledge that I wasn't so alone. She had my back. She supported me in this mad world, and I was there for her.

That's what friends were, so I wanted more.

I was ready to admit it to her. The feelings I had for her went beyond anything I felt for any of my other friends, and I wanted to explore those.

All that mattered was that she knew how I felt.

It was like the chain that had been hanging around my neck, shrinking ever so slowly, fell to the ground. A sense of freedom I never knew existed became a real possibility. I could see us together. Sharing our lives and supporting each other through it all, the highs and lows. Hugging her after winning a game, kissing her after she had a long day at work, merging into one unit.

How could it be I'd never seen it before? That was what people chased after. It wasn't the thrill of a new romance or the immediate gratification of physical intimacy. It was the in-between. The mundane. Wanting to share those ordinary moments with someone else. Knowing there was someone who cared.

I glanced back into the stands as I scooted down the bench to make room for the incoming line. Viv was smiling at something Taylor said to her, looking radiant as ever in the dim lights. She was beautiful. Stunning, actually. I expected to be intimidated when I first saw her, but that wasn't her nature. She was too warm, too open for anyone to feel that way.

She was the kind of person I longed to be. She gave me the courage and strength to try harder.

Now the game needed to hurry and end so I could see her

and tell her everything, but we still had seven minutes of playing time plus showering, changing, and any press. Each second felt like a minute. I only had one more rotation in before the final buzzer rang and we celebrated our win.

I hurried through the motions of getting ready, keeping an eye on my phone to track the time and if she texted me.

The hall was packed with women from the Pride and reporters. I weaved a path to Jess while scanning the sea of faces.

"Hey, great job tonight!" Jess said when I was in front of her.

"Thanks, we seem to be finding our rhythm together."

She grinned. "Did you see Lance? Is he close?"

"I think he was just getting dressed." I glanced around again.

"Viv already left. She said she couldn't come out with us tonight. She has a big meeting in the morning and wanted to get to bed so she could get up early."

"Oh." I tried not to show my disappointment but failed. She patted my arm. "She said to tell you how impressed she was and that she's proud she got to wear your number."

I smiled and thanked her.

Now that I knew she was gone, I was more than ready to get home. As pumped as I'd been just moments before, I was suddenly exhausted. The team had away games for the next week, so I wouldn't get a chance to talk to Vivi in person until we got back.

Seven days without telling her how I felt about her sounded impossible. I couldn't keep this in for that long. I wanted to tell her and see her reaction. Good or bad, I couldn't wait that long to find out. I'd go crazy by day three.

I debated heading over to her place now, but it was already nearing ten-thirty and I didn't want to wake her up. Our flight didn't leave until one tomorrow, so I could talk to her in the morning after her meeting. Maybe go by her office. Was that too forward or inappropriate? I'd never had a traditional job, so I wasn't quite sure how to navigate an office situation.

My head was spinning, and the likelihood of me making a sound decision was not so great. I'd go home and sleep and see what I came up with in the morning.

After tossing and turning most of the night, I finally got out of bed and went for a run just to burn time until it was a decent enough hour to call someone.

The plan I settled on hinged on one thing. I was going to call Kerry and see if Vivi had time this morning, after her meeting, to see me so I could surprise her. If she said yes, then I'd go in. If she said no, then I'd find a way to be patient until I got back.

When I got home, I took my time showering and eating breakfast to burn more time. Right at nine, I called their office and asked for Kerry.

"Kerry Hyatt," she answered in a professional voice.

"Hey, it's Parker. Garrison." I flinched. "Vivi's friend."

She laughed. "Yes, Parker, I know who you are."

"Oh, right. Okay."

"What can I do for you?"

I could hear typing in the background and was reminded I was interrupting her so I needed to get on with it.

"Would you happen to know if Vivi has any free time this morning? Before noon?" Hopefully sooner than that if I wanted to talk to her for longer than a minute before leaving for the airport.

"Let me check." There were some clicking sounds, then she hummed. "Her meeting goes until ten-thirty, then she usually meets with Jonathan right after to go over any notes or follow-up items." She paused again. "Then a meeting at eleven, but it should only go until eleven-thirty. I think you'd be safe to come then. She'll be free until an afternoon meeting."

I let out my breath. This was going to work. "Thanks, Kerry. I'll be by later."

"No problem. You can ask for me at the receptionist's desk, and I'll walk you over to her so you can surprise her if you want."

I hadn't thought that far ahead. "That would be great."

"She really likes the Santa Fe salad from the market cafe on the corner near our building. I happen to know she forgot to bring lunch today."

I smiled. "And is that a salad you also enjoy?"

"Oh yes, as a matter of fact," she replied.

"Perfect, thanks again."

I ended the call with more confidence than I probably had a right to have, but I had a plan. Steps to take. Now, all that was left was figuring out exactly what I was going to say.

It would likely depend on the situation. Would we be alone? Was Kerry going to stay around? How much time would Vivi actually have to talk to me? I needed to come up with options so I didn't stand there staring at her with a to-go box in my hands.

I fell back on the couch and covered my eyes with my arm. Why did getting on the ice in front of tens of thousands, if not hundreds, of people while an opposing team actively tried to take me down not bother me at all, but telling the girl I liked how I felt seemed impossible?

19

VIVIAN

I was rolling out my shoulders in a weak attempt to loosen my muscles and help relieve my stress headache. There was nothing like the days that started the instant you stepped off the elevator and didn't let you come up for air until you left at night.

This wasn't at all how my day was supposed to go. I was prepped and ready for the board meeting this morning. I had every base covered, and it went off marvelously. Jonathan was in a great mood and decided to reward everyone's efforts by telling me to order in breakfast. With zero notice.

I scrambled to make that happen while taking notes on the meeting for him to review after, as well as coordinating with the people in my next meeting since the board was taking their sweet time catching up with one another rather than getting through the agenda points.

It was great. They were happy because the company was exceeding goals and came in under budget and on time on the last major product. They wanted to celebrate, and it fell on me to make it happen.

There were only a dozen or so issues with that. Mostly,

mine. We'd gone over our time, not that anyone was going to complain about that when food was involved. My eleven o'clock meeting was supposed to begin in less than five minutes but there was no end to this on the horizon, so I had to message everyone in that meeting to make sure the team knew to go on without me and delegated the note-taking and task management to someone else.

At least I had Kerry available to run things behind the scenes. She went to pick up the breakfast order and brought it into the conference room for our guests, then ducked out and double-checked that my other meeting was in fact taking place as it should.

She messaged me updates on what was going on outside the ever-shrinking four walls of this room.

Only four people had asked about Jonathan and tried to get time with him so far. She was writing names and messages down for me, as well as taking the calls that redirected from my phone.

Once upon a time, she and I used to both attend these larger meetings, but the hours of damage control it cost us after led to us presenting the idea to our bosses of alternating meeting attendance. As much as that helped, it would have been nice to be able to skip these entirely. I didn't have much interest in listening to rich men talking about how much richer they were getting.

Jonathan was almost halfway through his presentation, I knew because I created it, and I was fully panicking. I didn't have the time to be in here. I shuffled things around for the morning but I had responsibilities screaming my name from my desk, but standing up and leaving wasn't an option. I'd have to do my best to multitask from my tablet.

Kerry sent me a message asking how much longer I expected this to take, and I replied with *infinitely*. There was no end in sight. At this point, I'd be putting in a lunch order too.

My head was killing me, but my water bottle and any medicine I had with me were at my desk. Maybe I could excuse myself and sneak away for just a minute. It wasn't like I needed to hear this information. I had it nearly memorized.

Another message appeared at the top of the screen. Kerry asking if I could come out for a minute.

If she was asking, it had to be important.

I checked that everyone's attention was forward, away from me, and got up as quietly as possible. I closed the door behind me and took a few silent steps before letting out a heavy sigh.

"That bad?" Kerry asked standing next to my desk.

I nodded and rummaged through my purse looking for pain killers. "And I've got a raging headache on top of it all."

"Oh no. That's the absolute worst." She glanced away. "You have a visitor."

I looked around and saw Parker walking toward us. My jaw nearly dropped.

"What are you doing here? Is everything okay?" I rushed out the words.

"Yeah, it's fine." He gave me a half-smile. "Kerry told me you're busy so I won't keep you long."

Kerry winked and walked away leaving the two of us alone.

"It wasn't supposed to be such a crazy day, but . . ." I trailed off, too tired to try to explain.

"I brought you lunch. A Santa Fe salad from the corner place."

My mouth instantly watered. "Really? Thank you. That's exactly what I need to look forward to if I'm going to survive this meeting."

He grinned. "I wish there was more I could do to help."

I waved him off. "I'll survive."

"So…" He paused, and I realized he probably didn't come just to bring me lunch. "I'm heading to the airport now. We'll be gone for a week."

Right. Some of the girls mentioned their away games, but it didn't click with me they would be gone for that long in one stretch. "That's kind of a long time."

He nodded. "It's one of the longer trips."

"I'm sorry. I didn't realize it, otherwise I would have waited to see you after the game last night."

Was that why he was here?

"I understand." He stared at the ground. "I just didn't want to go without saying bye, in person."

My chest hurt, it felt so full. He really did come here to see me. To say goodbye.

"Thanks for coming. I'm glad I got to see you."

He met my eyes, and there was a flicker of emotion I couldn't quite identify. "I won't keep you." He stepped forward, and I realized almost too late that he was going to hug me. I wrapped my arms around his waist and rested my head against his chest.

"I'll miss you," he whispered, and I held his eyes.

"I'll miss you too." I stepped back and tried to seem happy, but it suddenly felt like this was bigger than him being gone for a week. This was a pivotal moment when things changed.

He went to turn, but I grabbed his hand. "I don't know what your schedule is like on the road, but call or text me when you can. Okay?"

He scanned my face, a smile tugging at his lips. "Okay."

I let him go and watched as he walked away. A few people stared as he headed to the elevator, and I wondered if they recognized him or if they were curious about who showed up to see me.

I could wonder about that later. I grabbed my tablet and hurried back into the meeting room. Not a single head turned my way as I settled back into my seat. Jonathan had only made it through two slides in my absence, but I wasn't so bothered anymore. The meeting could last as long as they wanted. Parker came to see me. He came to say goodbye because he didn't want to leave without saying it. In person.

I couldn't believe it.

Kerry sent me a long string of heart-eye emojis, but I didn't respond.

Parker's visit was a kink in my plan. He wasn't supposed to appear the moment I needed him, like some sort of super-hero. It was almost enough to make me text Mitch and tell him to cancel the blind date he set up. Almost.

E zra, Mitch's friend from the boxing gym, sent me the directions for the local sports bar we were meeting at. When I told him I was down for what-ever he wanted to do, the last thing I expected was for him to recommend watching the Fury game together.

I should have realized then that the universe was screaming a message to me. I was too proud or determined or just plain stupid to listen.

The establishment—I couldn't think of a better word to describe it—was in a part of downtown that I'd never been. There wasn't necessarily a seedy side of Salt Lake City, espe-cially compared to other major cities, but if there was, this would be it. At least I held firm in my insistence that I meet him there. Jess let me borrow her car. More accurately, she insisted I take it because she didn't want me relying on a taxi or car service in case things went badly.

As much as we both trusted Mitch and his word, neither of us was taking chances. I texted her the address and told her when I arrived. She would check in throughout the night, and if I didn't reply to two messages in a row, she would come to find me.

It was going to be fine. Just fine. I repeated that to myself as I got out and walked through the old, rotting wood door. The inside was shocking. I actually stopped in the middle of the entry as the heavy door slammed into me.

It was bright and clean and crowded. Not at all like the rundown exterior. Was this some kind of joke? A way to dissuade customers? But why would anyone do that? How could a business survive?

"Vivian?" a male voice called from the farthest corner. A large man stood next to a tall table with his arm in the air.

I avoided the eyes watching me cross the room, my steps faltering when I realized I had a decision to make. How should I greet him? A hug? Handshake? Fist bump?

This wasn't only my first date in a long time, but my first blind date in years. There wasn't a rulebook for how to make it through awkward situations. I would know. I've looked.

"Hey, Vivian, so nice to meet you." Ezra made the choice for me when he wrapped his burly arms around me and squeezed about ten percent too tight.

I patted his back twice and tried to pull away but he held on. The thick scent of motor oil and body odor hit me with a force no one could have prepared for.

I stepped out of his arms and slid onto the chair across from him, forcing my smile to hold in place. This was one of Mitch's best friends. I couldn't be rude, especially when they were both doing me a favor.

"Have you been here before?" he asked.

"No, I haven't." I looked around for a menu but there was only a small paper listing the monthly beer specials.

"They've got all the best drafts, but I like them for their local selection." He began listing off the selection, but after the first four or five, I stopped listening. I wasn't much of a beer drinker, or a fan of anything that was a *required* taste. If I had to try something a dozen times to get used to it, or lie to myself about it tasting good, then I wasn't a fan.

Plus, it was a Thursday, and as a rule, I didn't drink on weeknights.

"Any food recommendations?" I asked.

"Oh man, their wings are incredible." He then switched to listing the sauce options.

A nearby waitress caught my eye, and I gave a small nod hoping she would catch on. She turned and came to our table. "Would you guys like to order anything?"

"A dozen blazing buffalo wings for me, and another pint when you have a chance." He tapped the rim of the almost empty glass.

She gave me a sympathetic smile. "And for you?"

Wings were a disastrous date food, the mess alone would give me anxiety, then there was the munching on bones to contend with. "Do you have a boneless option?"

"Sorry, no. We have wings, nachos, onion rings, and motz sticks."

"I'm tellin' you the wings are the way to go." Ezra slapped the table with a wide grin.

Oh boy. "I'll just have a Diet Coke, please."

"Coming right up." The waitress spun and headed to the bar.

"You're missing out," he commented. "So, Mitch tells me you're new to the world of hockey. What did you watch before?"

I hesitated. "Like what shows or movies?"

"No, what sport?"

I shook my head. "I've never really been into sports before now."

He cocked his head. "Not football?"

"Nope."

"Baseball?"

"No."

"Basketball?"

"Not that either."

"Huh." He seemed genuinely perplexed. "So no boxing then, either."

"No, I've never seen a single match."

"That's too bad." He took a big gulp of his drink and smacked his lips. "Nothing better than finishing a long day with a good beer and a good game."

I had no idea what to say. Was this the right person? Mitch really thought he and I would get along? Five minutes together, and I was ready to leave.

My phone vibrated in my pocket, and I pulled it out enough to text Jess that I was alive. Ezra didn't even notice. He was still talking about all the benefits of sports programming.

"What do you do for a living?" I interrupted. I didn't want to be rude, but if this night could be salvaged, I was going to try.

"I'm a warehouse manager, but my passion is restoring old motorcycles. I was actually working on an Indian before I came over."

That explained the oil smell.

"One day I want to open my own shop."

"That's very cool. How did you get--"

"Game's on!" he shouted, cutting me off. He was staring behind me, and I looked over my shoulder to see a massive flat screen with Parker's face in the center.

Was the universe against me? They were talking about the rising star of the Fury and what they expected to see from him tonight.

Was it a sign?

Maybe this was the universe's way of screaming at me that all I needed and wanted was right in front of my face. Literally.

My next two attempts at conversation were ignored since Ezra was so enthralled by the game, screaming and cursing at the refs as if they could hear him in Florida. Finally, I gave up and placed a five-dollar bill on the table for my drink.

"It was nice meeting you, but I have an early day tomorrow."

It was only seven, but I didn't care.

He grunted as the only acknowledgment he might have heard me, and I picked up my purse and hurried out.

This was all a waste. A huge mistake.

I didn't need to date someone else to know how I felt. I didn't need to see how awful things could be to know how lucky I was to have Parker in my life.

My heart already knew what my mind was just now seeing. I'd fallen for my friend.

20

PARKER

Despite talking to Vivi each day, I missed her. A few texts and a short phone call weren't enough. I wanted to see her and hold her as I had at her office. It was ridiculous how much I enjoyed a simple hug. The feeling of her body pressed against mine was familiar and comforting. In just a few weeks she went from a complete stranger to someone I couldn't imagine life without.

I hated that I didn't get the chance to talk to her about how I was feeling before I left, but the timing wasn't right. For whatever reason, fate or the universe didn't want me to tell her that day. Admitting how much I liked her, then turning around and leaving for a week probably wouldn't have been any easier than holding it in. That wouldn't really have been fair to either of us. I couldn't dump that on her, at her place of work, then fly across the country for a week without giving her the time to absorb the information and react.

It was a good thing. A solid relationship wasn't something that should be rushed. I wanted to take her to a romantic dinner, or at least on some sort of proper date, before telling her I was falling for her.

"Quit pouting, Garrison." Lance jabbed his elbow into my ribs as he passed me in the hall of the training arena we were using.

I ignored him and continued to the locker room. I wanted to shower and get back to the hotel to rest before the game tonight. I didn't bother arguing with him. I knew I'd been a downer, but I didn't have it in me to waste energy on faking it. I needed to save it for the game.

"You heading back?" Mitch asked after I cleaned off and changed into warm-ups.

"Yeah, want to walk with me?" I asked while hefting my bag onto my shoulder.

"Sure." He picked up his bag, and we headed out. The hotel we were staying in was conveniently close to the training area, but it was a twenty-minute drive to the arena downtown where we'd play tonight.

"You okay?" he asked once we were outside.

The warm Tampa sun was a welcome reprieve from the snowy, gray skies of Salt Lake. It made the five-minute walk far more desirable than waiting for the infrequent shuttle to come pick us up.

"You've been extra quiet lately," Mitch said. "Is everything okay?"

I didn't answer immediately. Yes, everything was okay in general. Nothing was technically wrong. I was healthy, strong, and feeling good after that practice. I was just in a bummer mood. I was pouting, and so grateful Lance pointed that out to me. I'd have to return the favor next time he missed Jess.

"I've been thinking about Vivi," I finally admitted.

"Yeah? What about her?" He pressed the button to change the walk signal.

"I really like her. I know it's kind of fast. I mean, we've only known each other for a little while, but I think I've had feelings for her from the moment we met."

He glanced at me. "Like love at first sight?"

I shrugged. "I don't know if I believe in that. A least, I didn't before. But maybe that's what this is. It wasn't like I saw her and thought, bam! That's her. It was more like a pull, something dragging me toward her, and the more I got to know her the stronger it got."

"I thought you were going to tell her how you felt."

"I was, but when I tried, it didn't work out. Then we left town, and I didn't want to have this conversation over the phone."

He nodded and rubbed his chin. "But your feelings haven't changed?"

"No, but maybe it was a sign that I didn't get the chance to tell her. Maybe I'm not supposed to."

"I should probably tell you something." His voice lowered.

My stomach dropped to the ground. He didn't sound like he was about to tell me good news. "What?"

We were at the entrance to the hotel, but he stopped a few yards away from the door. "Vivi asked a favor of me."

I narrowed my eyes. "What kind of favor?"

"She asked me to set her up with one of my friends."

His words didn't make sense. "What do you mean, set up?"

"She asked me to set her up on a blind date."

He might have thought that explained it better, but my mind was trying to bat the words away. I inhaled slowly before letting out a sigh. "Did you?"

"Yeah," he admitted before looking at the ground. "It happened last night."

My jaw was so tight, I thought I might crack a molar. I

hummed, not able to speak. Why would he do that? How could he betray me like that? Not only did he have to live with me, but I thought we were friends. Apparently, he didn't think so.

"Look, I didn't want to go through with it, but she was adamant it was what she wanted."

I turned away, staring out at the street. Why would she want to date another guy? Was she not interested in me? Had I misread all the signs? I thought she might feel the same way about me. Was I just seeing what I wanted to? Projecting my emotions and thoughts onto her?

"Thanks for telling me. I'm glad I didn't embarrass myself." My shoulders slumped, and I was suddenly exhausted. I did appreciate that he was being honest with me, but I wished he could have at least waited until after tonight's game.

"Stop." He reached out and tugged on my arm to get me to face him. "What are you feeling right now?"

I glared at him. "Nothing good."

He held my gaze, unwavering. "Doesn't that tell you something?"

I shook my head. "Not really."

"Are you angry at me for setting her up?"

I nodded.

"Are you angry at her for going out with another guy?"

I nodded again.

"Tell me why." He kept his gaze locked on mine.

"Because I really like her, and she doesn't feel the same. I want to date her. I want to be the one she wants to go out with, but she wants to date strangers. Also, because she trusted you and went to you, rather than talking to me."

"That doesn't sound as much like anger as it does jealousy." He raised a brow. "Is there a chance you're not as angry as you think? It's okay to be hurt. Be mad at me for participating, but put that aside. Are you really angry with her, or are you jealous of the other guy?"

I was all of the above. "I'm pretty angry, but I am hurt you would do that to me. And I am jealous."

"I'm sorry, but I was trying to help."

I flinched. "Her or me?"

"Both." He shrugged. "I'm not going to insert myself even deeper in this mess, but I think you should really think about what you're feeling and why. Then you should talk to her."

"I'm not sure I want to." It felt like my body deflated. Like I was a shell of who I'd been just minutes before.

"Parker, give yourself time to cool off and process. Once you really think it over, talk to her. If you don't think you can without losing it, then come talk to me."

I walked away without replying. I didn't want to listen to his advice, even if it was solid. I didn't want to be around him at all. The betrayal I felt was blurred between both him and Vivi. Why did she want to go on a blind date? She never mentioned wanting to date anyone. I'd been blindsided. Slapped across the face by the revelation.

And Mitch.

Why did he say yes? Why had he gone through with it? Why hadn't he warned me before now?

Each question I had just made me sicker. When I got to my room, I dropped my bag on the ground and fell face-first onto the bed. I knew I wouldn't be able to sleep, even for an hour or two, but I didn't want to do anything else but lie there and try to figure out how I'd been so completely wrong about Viv.

I never in a million years would have predicted that she wanted to date someone else. I thought that was the direction we were headed. How could I have been so stupid? I wasn't experienced with women or dating or relationships, but I didn't know I was this off.

The worst part was how much I physically hurt. My chest was tight, my stomach rolled, every limb felt heavy. Was this heartbreak? It had to be.

What an idiot. I was immensely grateful I hadn't told her how I felt. How humiliating would that have been? I'd never be able to look her in the eyes again if I'd stood there while she told me that she only saw me as a friend after I poured my heart out to her.

Maybe the universe was watching out for me. I thought it was working against me, but now it seemed like it had my back. More so than my roommate. I wasn't sure I could consider him a friend after this.

I let my anger and hurt simmer until it was time to get up and change into my suit. I pulled on my jacket and slipped on sunglasses. I didn't want anyone taking a picture of me looking as dejected as my face currently depicted.

"Hey, you ready for this, Garrison? You were looking good earlier." Brandon and Lance were walking down the hall and waited for me to catch up.

This was perfect. I needed a distraction, and being around them wouldn't let me slip back into my pity party.

"Yeah, I'm feeling good." It was a lie right now, but within a few minutes, I'd be back to normal. I was good at compartmentalizing. I could slip out of my normal life and into player-mode like flipping a switch after this many years of practice.

"Should we knock and get Mitch?" Brandon asked. "I think he's the only other one on this floor." He looked from the row of doors then to me. He probably expected me to know which was his, us being friends and all, but I just shrugged.

"We can wait for him downstairs." I kept walking to the elevator.

Lance stayed at my side. "Did you get a chance to watch

the videos Coach sent? The Gators have used the same play in their last four games, heavy on the defense. I think they're starting to rely on that, so you guys have to watch for openings."

I agreed. "Yeah, I wondered why they were relying so heavily on defense. I don't think their injured list is that bad."

"Me either," Brandon added from behind us. We stepped onto the elevator, and he pressed the button for the lobby.

"Have you heard any talk about their offense being weak this season?" I asked. The Gators hadn't been playing this way for very long, maybe only a few weeks before my trade.

"Not really. Maybe this is a new strategy they're trying," Brandon replied.

"Nah, I think it's their goalie," Lance said. "He's a young guy, only been in the league for one season, but he's the best they've got. I think they're trying to keep the other team from even entering their zone."

I huffed out a laugh. "Well then. There's their weakness."

Brandon smirked. "Let's spread the word."

Lance chuckled as we walked out, looking even cockier than normal. He walked up to Hartman and Schultz and began talking to them.

"I'll talk to them." Brandon nodded toward Brassard, Fisher, and Koslov.

I was about to walk toward Jason, Jake, and Derek until I realized Mitch was with them. I couldn't avoid him forever, especially not if I wanted to keep what happened between us and not have the entire team know about my embarrassment, but I could delay speaking to him for a while longer. I sighed and headed over to Murray and Letang.

21

VIVIAN

ll I wanted was dinner and a bath. If Jess wasn't home to discourage me from ordering take-out for the third time this week, then I was going to call my trusty Thai restaurant and have them bring my favorite noodles while I soaked away the day.

Things weren't normally this busy for us at work, especially in the first quarter of the year, but with all the growth we'd had, the board thought we should move forward with full force toward early product launches in the next few months.

I tried to get Jonathan to see that things were working so well because we found a process that worked. Our engineers and designers were working at a comfortable pace that allowed them to yield amazing results. Pushing them now would ruin all of that. When was the last time a great product, or even an upgrade, was released under pressure? That was when mistakes were made. That's when corners were cut and people grew frustrated.

The board wasn't in the office, ever. They didn't know that the atmosphere we'd created allowed the teams to thrive. They weren't around to watch exhaustion take over. They didn't see even the happiest of employees grow resentful if their work hours got too long.

Nothing I said worked. Jonathan was under pressure from the board to produce. He should have stood up for his teams. He should have been their advocate and pushed back on the demands. His loyal employees had built the company to what it now was, success and all, and they deserved for him to have their backs.

It was disappointing, to say the least. Even though I ran things behind the scenes, coordinated projects, and kept things on track, at the end of the day, I was just his assistant. He was the big boss. He was the decision-maker. I wasn't there to have an opinion or give him advice.

Things were fine, for now. No one would feel the impact for a few weeks, at least. But the stress would set in. Maybe I could find a solution that Jonathan would agree to before then. This was the first thing I'd felt passionate about in a while here. I wanted to maintain the culture of this company and make sure the people here felt valued.

The apartment was silent when I walked in. Jess mentioned a wedding coming up, but I wasn't sure of its exact date. She must've been working on it tonight.

I ordered dinner online and had forty minutes before it was expected to be delivered, so I went to my room and started the water in the tub. Lavender or eucalyptus? Both sounded divine, but did I need relaxation or relief more? I tried to roll my tight shoulders. Eucalyptus it was.

Just as I reached to pull my shirt off, the doorbell rang. I checked my phone, but only six minutes passed. There was no way my food was already here. The tub was only a quarter full, but I turned off the water and hurried to the door.

I gasped when I opened it to see Parker waiting. He was

in very well-fitting jeans and a tight t-shirt and smelled like men's body wash. He was much better than the hot bath I'd been waiting for.

"You're back?" Did I have my days mixed up? I could have sworn the team was coming back tomorrow.

"Yeah, we got back early." He looked around, waiting.

Oh right. "Come in." I opened the door wider, and he passed before I shut it.

"I probably should have called or at least texted first, but I wanted to talk to you in person." He glanced at me before crossing to the living room and sitting down.

Something was wrong. The way he carried himself. The tone of his voice. I didn't want to sit, so I leaned against the arm of the couch.

"What's going on?" Maybe something happened to his family. I watched the games, and they'd lost two but won their most recent. That didn't seem like something he would hold onto. No, this was something else.

"Mitch told me about your date."

Those were the last words I expected to come from his mouth. That sweet, gorgeous mouth I'd been thinking about all week.

The flash of panic passed, and I nearly broke out laughing. I moved some pillows and sat facing him. "It was with his friend from his boxing gym. I swear, it was the worst experience I've ever had. It looked like a total dive from the outside, but inside it was pretty nice. He smelled like oil and sweat, and I'm pretty sure he didn't bother showing before. He said he works on motorcycles in his off time which explains the oil smell, but he could have at least washed off. As if that wasn't the worst part, he just wanted to watch the game after we ordered. Oh, and they didn't have anything except fried bar food. I still don't know why he picked that place. Anyway, he barely said two words to me before his attention was sucked into the game." I chuckled.

He did not.

His focus was on his hands in his lap. "Why did you want to go out with him?"

I swallowed. Was he … mad? He was mad at me for going on a date? Since when was that a problem? None of my other *friends* cared.

"I wanted to see--"

"I just don't understand," he cut me off. "When Mitch told me, I thought he was joking."

He shook his head and sighed.

He was really upset. Over me going on a date.

My anger turned to confusion, then faded to understanding. He wasn't mad. He was jealous. I trailed my eyes up and down his body. I could see it now. The sag in his shoulders. How he wouldn't meet my eyes. His dejected tone. How long had he known? Was he like this for the whole trip?

Why didn't Mitch warn me? He could have at least given me a heads up that he'd spilled the beans so I could prepare.

"Parker," I started, but he lifted his head and the pained look in his eyes made me stop.

"The day I came to your office, I wanted to talk to you. I had a whole speech planned, but you were so busy and I didn't want to take too much time or distract you." He blew out a breath. "I still can't decide if that was a blessing or not."

"What do you mean?" My heart was racing. He'd come to talk to me? About what?

"At first I thought having to wait to tell you was just another roadblock. Some obstacle to overcome, but now I think it was a sign. A break to force me to rethink things."

No. That sounded horrible. The opposite of what I wanted.

"Please, let me explain."

His head shot up. "Explain? You don't need to tell me anything. We're just friends. You're free to date anyone you want."

"That's the thing. I don't want to." I rushed out the words before he could stop me. "That's what I'm trying to tell you. The date was so bad, and I turned to look at the screen and they were talking about you. I saw your picture and realized how dumb it was that I was even there, so I left."

He blinked and met my eyes. "You left?"

"I was only there long enough to take a few sips of my Diet Coke."

His brows pulled together. "Does Mitch know that?"

I nodded. "I called him on my way home and asked him what on earth he'd been thinking. The whole point of that date was to treat it as an experiment, but I swear he blew it on purpose."

He didn't say anything. Just stared at a spot over my shoulder. "He didn't tell me that."

I groaned. "His friend was truly terrible, but it worked."

His eyes flashed to mine. "What?"

"The experiment." I mustered all my courage. I'd waited so long, okay a few days, for him to get home so I could tell him in person.

"What do you mean?"

"I went on that date because I was confused." I paused. "No that's not completely true. I was scared."

He shifted. "What were you scared of?"

I swallowed. This was it. Time to be brave. "Of my feelings." I waited for a breath for him to say something but he stayed silent. "I realized I was starting to feel more for you than just friendship, and it kind of freaked me out. The more I allowed myself to acknowledge those emotions, the further from friends they became. Things with us are new, and I like spending time with you. I was scared that if I told you, I'd ruin things."

"So you went on a date with someone else?" he asked, his expression wounded.

"When you repeat it back like that, it sounds pretty stupid." His brow rose. "I thought if I went out with someone else, I would be able to compare how I felt around them to how I feel around you and it would clarify things. I told myself it was the shiny-new-toy excitement of having you in my life that I was feeling, not anything real. I tried to convince myself that I'd feel the same thing with any new guy, but I quickly learned that's not the case."

He took in a long breath. "So these feelings?"

I bit my lip as my face warmed.

"You're sure about them?" he asked.

"Yes, Parker. I'm certain."

He looked down again. I scooted closer to him, needing to take his hand. I hesitated, fearing he'd pull away, but his fingers slid through mine and he squeezed.

"I should have just told you, but I didn't want to lose what we were building," I admitted.

"Vivi." His voice was hoarse. "You're not going to lose me."

"But?" I asked. I could feel it hanging in in the air. This was where he'd let me down gently. The 'it's not you, but me' speech. When he'd tell me he only saw me as a friend.

"No buts. I couldn't stop thinking about you, even before the trip, but every second I was gone, I wished I was right here. I'm just as scared as you. I don't want to mess up what we have either. I'm not the best at opening up and letting people in, but it's different with you. Being with you is as easy as skating for me." He smiled. "That's super cheesy."

I traced his jaw with my finger. "It's perfect because that's how I feel. Minus the skating. I'm horrible at that, but being with you is effortless. I don't feel like I have to put on an act. You accept me the way I am."

He nodded. "I don't want you to change a thing."

That was the first time I remembered anyone ever saying that to me. My eyes burned, and I fought back the tears. "I'm so glad I met you."

"Me too." He scanned my face before leaning forward.

My heart nearly exploded from my chest when his lips touched mine. The relief and excitement and joy that filled me was almost too much. This was all I'd been wanting and thinking about for nearly two weeks, and it was finally happening.

His hand wrapped around the back of my neck, and I gripped the front of his shirt as he deepened the kiss.

He pulled back enough to touch his forehead to mine. "This is real, right?"

My cheeks were already aching from smiling.

"I want to take you on a proper date."

"Okay." I would agree to just about anything at that moment.

"Tonight?"

I was about to say yes when I remembered the food I'd ordered. It felt like a lifetime ago. The time *before.* Oh no. Was I going to be one of those sappy romantics that only remembered life after they met *the one*?

Whoa. I was getting ahead of myself. I liked him and he liked me, but it was far too soon to toss around *the one* and *happily ever after.*

"I ordered something, but we can go after it gets delivered."

"Sorry I interrupted." He sounded genuinely remorseful.

"I would definitely rather have had this talk than the bath I was planning on."

"Wow, that's quite the compliment."

I laughed. "It really is. I guess you know where you are on my list now."

"Not really." He smiled.

"I'll only tell you that you bumped baths out of the top three."

"Huh, so there are two things you love more than me?" He flinched. "I mean, not that you love me." I laughed, hiding my sudden spike of anxiety, and he covered his eyes. "I walked myself into that."

Love? It was such a huge word. It held more weight than simply liking someone. It was a declaration. It was an action. A promise.

I wanted to be one-hundred percent certain I was ready for everything it meant before I said those three words to him.

22

PARKER

The next day I went through the motions of eating breakfast and getting ready for practice like I was floating. I'd never felt so light before. I expected last night to go in a completely different direction. I walked into Viv's place, expecting her to tell me it was none of my business who she dated or that she really liked the new guy. The chance that she might actually feel the same way about me after what Mitch told me never crossed my mind.

If anything, I was expecting her to tell me that we could stay friends just from a distance.

Instead, my world changed.

She wanted me. She liked me. Not some random friend of Mitch's. Nope. Me. And not because of who I was. She didn't care about the hockey stuff. She supported me, but I could have been anything and she would still like me. I wasn't sure I'd ever get used to this feeling, and I was even less sure I wanted to.

This could be my new normal and I would be very much okay with that.

"You're cheerful," Mitch grumbled as he walked into the kitchen in search of his morning cup of coffee.

"I had an interesting conversation last night."

"Oh?" he replied in a bored tone while pulling his creamer from the fridge.

"Yeah, I went over to see Vivi."

"So that's where you went." He poured a few splashes in and returned the bottle.

"It seems like there's something you forgot to tell me." I leaned against the counter, blocking his exit.

He tightened the lid on his travel mug before meeting my gaze. "I don't know what you mean."

I narrowed my eyes. "How about the fact that the date lasted less than ten minutes?"

He smiled, but quickly cleared his throat and it disappeared. "Right, small detail."

"Or that you set her up with some sort of smelly motorhead."

He took a sip of his drink and shrugged.

"At first, I just questioned your judgment and the friends you keep, but then a thought struck me. I know you're not that incompetent, and if you really wanted to, you could have found a great guy to set her up with. But you didn't. On purpose."

He looked everywhere but at me. "I don't know what you mean."

I stepped closer. "You sabotaged her."

His brows shot up. "I did not!"

I grinned. "You did, and you did it for me."

He tipped his chin. "Not everything is about you, Garrison."

"Fine, you did it for us."

He didn't argue that time.

"So is he actually that terrible, or did you pay him to really push her over the edge?"

Finally, he cracked. He let out a laugh. "I told him not to shower. He tried to argue with me since he was coaching at the gym, then had a Harley he was working on for a buddy, but I told him to just go. It was his idea to go to that bar. He said it was the worst date place he could think of. It was a bit of a joint effort with the other guys at the gym to come up with watching your game, but it was sheer luck that they happened to be doing a feature on you that night."

I rubbed my face. Part of me wanted to punch him, while the other wanted to give him a hug.

"That's like evil genius status." I felt bad complimenting him, but it had all worked out for my benefit.

"Ezra really got into the role. He called me, barely able to contain himself. He felt awful but also thought it was one of the funniest things he'd ever done. He said even if he wasn't acting like a disgusting jerk, it was clear that her mind was somewhere else. Then she saw you on the screen, and it was like a switch flipped and she just left."

I tried not to let that go to my head, but it made me feel pretty good.

"I'm sorry I got involved, but she came to me really confused and thought this was what she needed to sort out her feelings. I already knew how you felt about her, so I just twisted things a bit to make sure she got her head straight too."

I let out a laugh. "You should have told me earlier. I wouldn't have spent the past few days mad at you."

He shrugged. "When I saw how you reacted in Florida, I knew it was real for you too, but when you questioned it. . . I panicked. I wanted to push you to admit to yourself how much you cared. That you didn't want her to be with anyone else."

"I didn't know you were such a matchmaker." I took a step back and went to pick up my bag near the door. "Let me know if I can ever return the favor."

He paused mid-step before nodding. "Sure thing."

"Let's get going. I was hoping we'd get the day off, but maybe we'll get lucky with a light practice."

"I doubt it. Hartman took the second loss personally. He's going to be after us until we make up those points."

We only dropped to the third spot in our division, and we had time to recover before playoffs, but he was right. Hartman wasn't captain because he took it easy. Each win and loss hit him harder than the rest of us. His determination to be the best kept the rest of us at the top of our game. You couldn't help but respect him, and the last thing any of us wanted was to disappoint him.

He wanted another championship, and he was going to get us there even if it killed us.

"There's no such thing as light practices for the Fury." Mitch clapped me on the shoulder before locking the door behind us. "That's what ice baths are for."

I chuckled, then thought of Vivi. I bet if I introduced her to ice baths, they'd fall even further down the list. Not that it would help me move up. I had to figure out what her first two loves were in order to knock them down. I didn't mind a challenge. All I wanted was to get to know her more and more. With enough time, I'd know everything she loved and hated. Her favorite memories and the ones that stung.

I wanted it all, but that was a part of the journey.

"Your smile's freaking me out," Mitch teased as we got into his car.

"I was thinking about Vivi."

"I figured." He pulled out of the garage and headed toward the arena. "I'm assuming I don't have to make the speech."

"Which one?"

"The one where I make it clear that if you hurt her in any way, I'll make you pay."

I swallowed. "Got it."

Mitch was one of the nicest guys on the team, once you got past the burly exterior, but I knew he could throw a punch as well, thanks to all the time he spent at the boxing gym. He'd live up to his words and make me regret ever meeting Vivi if I messed up.

We predicted correctly. Practice was grueling. Even though Coach Rust and Romney were on the ice with us, they let Hartman take the lead. He pushed us to go harder and faster and longer than any of us thought possible. We were exhausted after a long streak of away games, but he continued to punish us for the two points lost. Schultz and Letang, even Brassard, tried to get him to take it down a notch after an hour, but he wouldn't listen.

It reminded me of my high school days when we'd run drills until we crumbled as a part of conditioning.

I refused to be the first to fall behind. Or second. Not even the third. Maybe after four or five others slowed down, I'd allow myself to show weakness. I was still proving myself, and while I didn't feel the need to show off and come out at the head of the pack, I certainly wasn't going to be the weakest link.

My hair was dripping sweat into my eyes, and my face itched under my beard. I wanted this torture to end.

We went another fifteen minutes before a whistle blew. Coach Rust stepped forward, calling it a day.

Hartman glared at him but didn't argue.

"If we don't stop now, none of you will be able to play tomorrow." Rust addressed us but kept his eyes on our captain. "Hit the showers. You guys stink."

A few of the guys laughed, but that would take up any

remaining energy I had in my body, and I still had to make it down the hall to the locker room.

I sat on the closest bench and dropped my head into my hands.

"Here." Brandon handed me a water bottle, and I downed it without taking a breath.

"Thanks, man."

He fell into the spot next to me, and Murray strode toward us like he wasn't feeling the pain at all. "Chloe saw how hard we were going and has dinner ready at our place."

It wasn't an invitation so much as a statement so I just sat there, staring up at him, still marveling at how normal he was acting.

"She tell Syd?" Brandon huffed out.

"Yeah, she sent out the text." He shifted his attention to me. "Jess and Dani are picking Vivian up on their way over."

I wasn't sure what to do with that information. She was going to his house. For dinner.

"Do you need a ride?" Brandon asked, and I looked over to see him waiting for me.

"Oh, maybe. I came over with Mitch so I'll check to see if he's going." Huh, not only was I invited, but I was expected to attend.

Murray turned. "Hey, Dory! You coming?"

Mitch stopped with his shirt halfway off. "To your house? Sure."

"There you go." Murray patted my shoulder and walked away.

I was too stunned to react for a moment.

"Is that normal?" I asked Brandon.

"What?"

"The dinner?"

"Oh yeah. Usually once a week or so, one of us will host." He answered casually, as if this wasn't something some of the guys on the team seemed to obsess over. Okay, maybe it was just Lance and Mikey that felt like the parties had some elusive invitation.

"Better hurry and get ready, or all the good food will be gone," Schultz announced as he walked by.

"Really?" I started pulling off my wet clothing.

"No, Chloe orders enough for a small army. All the women do. There are leftovers for days after these. My boys love it when we have it at our house."

I smiled. I'd seen his twins around, and they seemed like sweet kids. "Will they be there tonight?"

"Yeah, they like to watch all the babies. It makes them feel so old and mature."

It was strange to think of most of these guys as husbands and fathers. I knew they all had lives outside of the team, but picturing Schultz holding a baby just seemed wrong.

After we got ready, I text Vivi to make sure she did have a ride. When she confirmed, Mitch and I headed out of downtown to the base of the mountains that bordered the city. Massive houses lined the bench, and he pointed out Letang's street, then Schultz's before turning into a cul-de-sac where he parked.

There were half a dozen other cars on the street, but I wasn't sure if Vivi was already there. I couldn't wait to see her.

"Are you ready for this?" Mitch asked.

"For dinner?" I shot him a questioning look. Was there something I needed to do to prepare for a meal?

"For your first official outing as a couple."

I froze. We hadn't really discussed our status or decided on a label. We liked each other and were planning on going on a date this weekend. Did that automatically mean we were a couple?

"Oh no. Did I break you?"

I shook my head. "No, I just hadn't thought about it."

Crap. Now I wanted to find her and talk to her before everyone else arrived and people started talking.

"Don't worry. The piranhas will circle for a while before they bite."

What was he talking about? I pulled out my phone and sent her a text, asking if she was here, before catching up to him on the steps leading to the front door.

"There he is!" Chloe beamed at me with a baby on her hip. "We've been waiting."

The rest of the women emerged from thin air. Oh no.

"No sudden movements," Mitch whispered. "They'll attack."

23

VIVIAN

Dani opened the door to Reese and Chloe's house without knocking, and Jess and I followed behind her. A group was gathered just inside, taking up most of the entryway and adjoining living room.

The three of us shared a look.

"This is the first time we've all been together to celebrate the newest Fury!" Chloe raised a glass in the air. Seeing her with her baby was like seeing your teacher outside of school. It felt wrong even though you knew it was a reality. I was so used to her as the take-no-crap, boss-woman that seeing this softer side of her made me pause.

"To Parker!" the group said together.

I scanned the faces, looking for him.

"Come on, you should be with him," Jess whispered.

She cut through the crowd and stopped next to him and Mitch.

"Hey." I reached for his arm.

He looked down at me, and relief washed over his face. "There you are."

"We missed something already?" I ask as Chloe moved closer.

"Hey, Viv." She gave me a side hug, and Callen, her baby, reached for me. "Oh, guess he has a new friend."

Then he was in my arms. "Oh." I shifted to hold him on my hip as she had. "Hi, bub."

He cooed at me and started jabbering away in baby talk. Just like that, I fell in love. He was ridiculously adorable and chunky, and Chloe was going to have to pry him away from me.

"I'll be back." She waved and disappeared to the back of the house.

"He's yours now," Mitch said with a small smile. "I've heard the guys complain about how the babies get dumped on them for the night."

"Fine with me." I grinned down at Callen.

"Can we talk?" Parker asked and led me down a hall before I could answer. I glanced over my shoulder at Mitch, but he just winked and turned away.

"What's going on?" I asked once he stopped.

"A few things, but the most pressing is something Mitch pointed out to me." He seemed stressed. "This is the first time we're attending a team activity together."

I swallowed. "Okay."

He looked at the ground, then Callen squeaked and Parker cooed at him. "I'm not sure if you've told anyone about us."

"Jess and Dani. I told them on the way over."

He blew out a breath. "What did you tell them?"

Why was he acting so strange? Was he having second thoughts? We only agreed to a date. Was I being presumptuous in thinking that meant more? Did he want to keep it between us? It seemed like Mitch knew about us.

"That we talked and both have feelings for each other, and that we're planning on going out this weekend."

He nodded. "That's what I said to Mitch."

"So, what's the problem?" I bounced Callen gently when he starting fussing.

"I just wanted to make sure we were on the same page."

I thought we were until this conversation. He was keeping something from me. Not saying something he was thinking.

"Which is?" I asked.

"I'm not sure." His shoulders slumped. "I don't know if this means we're a couple. I feel immature saying you're my girlfriend just because we told each other we like each other."

I grinned. "When you say it like that, it does seem like a very middle school thing to do."

"Exactly, and I'm pretty sure that was the last time I was in a relationship."

He laughed, and I wanted so badly to kiss him. We were both pretty hopeless when it came to this stuff.

"Well, I like you and don't want to date anyone else."

"Same," he agreed.

"Then we're exclusive," I offered. "That sounds a little bit more mature, like we're at a high school level at least."

He chuckled. "That's progress."

"How about we say we're dating, even though technically we haven't been on an official date."

"I brought you lunch," he pointed out.

"That's true, and we can count the double date with Kerry," I added. "Oh, and the night I ordered from the deli."

"Hey! There's three. That's definitely dating." There was a sparkle in his eye, and I decided it was my new goal to see that a whole lot more often.

"So, we're clear? We're dating? Things are new?"

He eyes lit. "Yes."

"That was the weirdest conversation I've ever heard. I can't believe my son had to witness that." Reese appeared out of nowhere and reached for Callen. I handed him over too stunned to speak.

"Can you keep what you heard to yourself?" Parker asked.

Reese eyed him. "Why should I?"

"Because I'm new to the team and don't want a nickname or reputation to come from this. Also, it's not just about me. I don't want Vivi dragged into whatever twisted joke the team comes up with."

Reese looked to his son, then back to Parker. "You're lucky he's here. I'll let this one go, but only because Callen is here to witness. I don't want him thinking his dad is anything but kind and merciful."

"Of course. I will let him know as soon as he understands those words." Parker stepped to the side so Reese and his son could pass.

Once we were alone again, Parker lowered his head to place a quick kiss on my lips. I didn't even get to savor the sensation before he pulled back and took my hand in his. "Let's do this."

We went back down the hall to where the group had dispersed into the living room, kitchen, and dining room. The majority of the main floor was open, so as soon as one person spotted us, it felt like everyone turned to see.

"Oh, there they are!" Emma said in a singsong voice. "The newest Fury couple!"

A few people cheered, and I had to force myself not to run or at least cover my face.

Parker waved his free hand like he was greeting fans. "Thank you. Thank you. We're glad to be here."

"You two are the cutest," Dani squealed. "I saw this coming. Didn't I, babe?" She turned to Jake, who nodded.

"Hey! I called it too!" Mikey shouted from across the room. "The night we set up the event, they both asked me about each other, and I said it was only a matter of time."

Lance stood. "I can confirm."

I turned my head into Parker's shoulder. This was too much attention for me. I didn't know how he was standing it.

"You all might have seen it coming, but I was the one that made it happen," Mitch boasted.

"Yeah right, Dory," Schultz challenged.

"I pushed them together. They each told me they had feelings for the other, and I may or may not have sabotaged one of Vivi's dates to make sure they realized they needed to stop admitting how they felt to other people and talk to one another."

My jaw dropped. "Wait, what do you mean you sabotaged my date?"

His face turned pink as he laughed. "You don't think my friends are really that bad, do you?"

I almost shivered at the thought of Ezra. He was gross and rude. A bit too gross and too rude.

"Oh my gosh. That was an act." How did I not see this sooner? I had no reason to think Mitch would trick me. I simply trusted him.

"Of course, it was. It took some conniving. Ezra is usually a much more put-together man, but he eventually got into the role."

I scrunched my nose. "I can't believe you."

He shrugged. "It worked better than I could have planned."

Someone laughed, then another, and I was reminded we had an audience. Almost the entire team and the Pride were watching us and enjoying the entertainment.

"That's great." I shook my head. "I'll consider forgiving you one day."

"You warned me about the Pride, but it was you we needed to watch out for," Parker said.

"Hey!" Chloe stepped forward with her hands on her hips. "What did he say about us?"

Mitch put his hands up in surrender. "Nothing."

"Liar," Parker called out.

The women turned to Mitch, and Kendall and Madi led them to corner him.

"You can't go around scaring people," Madi said.

Kendall crossed her arms. "Yeah, we just try to help."

Mitch looked across the room to Parker, eyes pleading for help, but he led me to the kitchen in the opposite direction of his roommate.

"That was pretty decent payback," I admitted. "I still might have to do something though. I can't believe I didn't realize it was a hoax."

Parker handed me a plate, and I put a slice of deep-dish pizza on it. "I didn't think he had it in him, but he's some sort of evil mastermind. Part of me is worried he'll end up joining the pride and they'll become unbeatable."

I giggled. "I can actually see that happening."

He picked up a slice as well as a brownie and lemon tart, then we headed to open seats at the dining room table with Taylor, Jason, Amelia, and Derek.

"So, who's next?" Taylor asked.

"Lucy and Colin. Obviously," Amelia said before taking a bite of pizza.

"No, Addi and Grant have been engaged for a while. They're next," Derek argued.

"What are you talking about?" Parker asked.

"Who's getting married next," Taylor said with a smile.

"It's not either of you guys?" I asked.

Derek's eyes widened.

"Maybe," Amelia wagged her brows. "If someone here would hurry up."

"There's no rush," Derek grumbled.

"It could be us." Taylor waved her engagement ring in the air. "But we haven't even picked a date yet."

"Why not?" I asked.

"Life's been busy," she replied, not sounding concerned.

"Yeah, maybe this summer," Jason suggested.

"Are you going to have Dani and Jess plan it?" Parker asked.

"As if we have any other choice." Taylor laughed. "They'd kill us or undermine our weddings if we didn't."

"What if you guys are next?" Amelia looked between me and Parker. "That would be exciting."

"It would definitely throw off some bets," Jason agreed.

"Yeah, I don't think so," I said.

"We've only really been on three dates," Parker said. "I think marriage is pretty far off."

But it was a possibility? That's what it sounded like. He didn't immediately shoot down the idea or say they were crazy for even considering it.

I wasn't anywhere near being ready for marriage, but I kind of loved how he handled that.

"Maybe one day." I looked up at him and he winked.

"One day." He grinned, and I knew in my heart that was a promise.

THANKS FOR READING!

Thanks for reading! I hope you enjoyed Parker and
Vivi's story!
Word of mouth is so important for authors to succeed. If you
enjoyed Game Misconduct, I'd love for you to leave a review
on Amazon!

Keep Reading,
Xoxo B

Next in the Series
Face Off

She's a single mom struggling to put together the pieces of her life, and he's watching his career crumble around him. They have everything to lose if one more thing goes wrong, and even though disaster strikes every time they meet they can't fight the pull to the other.

Mikey Dankowski is living his dream life, but can feel it slipping from his grasp. His performance on the ice is drawing attention from the coach for all the wrong reasons and his best friends haven't noticed. He's preparing for the meeting that could change his world when he runs into a woman that lives him wondering if there's more to life than hockey.

Holly Evans never imagined she'd be reentering the workforce after seven years of playing the perfect housewife, but she'll do anything to show her daughter how to be brave and independent. Her determination is unwavering, except for the obnoxious memory of the face of the man that nearly ruined her first day.

Will a string of awful encounters ruin their chances of seeing they're exactly what each other needs?

ALSO BY BRITTNEY MULLINER

ROMANCE

Utah Fury Hockey

Puck Drop (Reese and Chloe)

Match Penalty (Erik and Madeline)

Line Change (Noah and Colby)

Attaching Zone (Wyatt and Kendall)

Buzzer Beater (Colin and Lucy)

Open Net (Olli and Emma)

Full Strength (Grant and Addison)

Drop Pass (Nikolay and Elena)

Scoring Chance (Derrek and Amelia)

Penalty Kill (Brandon and Sydney)

Power Play (Jason and Taylor)

Center Ice (Jake and Dani)

Game Misconduct (Parker and Vivian)

Face Off (Mikey and Holly)

Snowflakes & Ice Skates (Lance and Jessica)

A Holiday Short Story to be read between Center Ice and Game Misconduct

Royals of Lochland

His Royal Request

His Royal Regret

Her Royal Rebellion

Young Adult

Begin Again Series

Begin Again

Live Again

Love Again (Coming Soon)

Charmed Series

Finding My Charming

Finding My Truth (Coming Soon)

Standalones

The Invisibles

ABOUT THE AUTHOR

Brittney Mulliner writes contemporary, young adult, and sports romance novels for readers of all ages. As a life-long avid reader, growing up, her parents would often take away her books to make her go play outside, but nothing could compare to the adventure of a good book. Born and raised in Southern California, she now lives in the Rocky Mountains with her husband and Goldendoodle, Freddie Mercury. She's a devout hockey fan, loves working out while listening to audiobooks, and is on a lifelong hunt for the best gluten-free cinnamon roll.

For exclusive content and the most up to date news, sign up for Brittney's newsletter at www.brittneymulliner.com

Find out more about Brittney and her books at
www.Brittneymulliner.com

Made in the USA
Middletown, DE
04 September 2021

47587661R00125